JULIANDRA

by Shawn Lewis Hill

JULIANDRA

Wordsmith Publishing
P.O. Box 282
Carmel, Maine 04419

Drafted, 2014
First Printing, 2015
Revised, 2016

ISBN-13: 978-0692388723 (Wordsmith Publishing)

ISBN-10: 0692388729

Cover artwork and design by Shawn Lewis Hill
Author photo by Shawn Lewis Hill

CONTENTS

PREFACE (AUTHOR'S THOUGHTS) IV

ACKNOWLEDGEMENTS V

INTRODUCTION 1

THE DAY BEFORE 4

THE MORNING 24

THE RECOVERY 34

THE REPEATING 42

THE CHANGE 55

THE FIRST TIME 67

THE QUESTIONS 77

THE ANSWERS 102

THE WAIT 116

THE SHOE 126

THE MEETING 132

THE HUNT 145

THE HOPE 164

PREFACE

I was inspired to write this book in order to tell a story I felt needed to be told, and to no longer keep it locked away within my imagination. After years of only being an idea, the decision was made to embark on the journey of becoming an author so those thoughts could be shared with the world.

You see, I believe that the majority of us alive today are romantics at heart, but get too caught up in the day to day formalities of existing within society, and that essential passion, that romance, becomes lost.

Our basic emotional needs are normally neglected, and so we attempt to fill that void with artificial and short lived joys, from buying new things, treating ourselves to a favorite food, altering our appearance, or even changing who we are; when truly, what we need is to embrace that which we were born to do. Love and be loved.

Without each other, life would have very little meaning. Just imagine being the only living being on earth.

Would you care what you looked like?

Would you take pride in anything you did or accomplished?

Would you strive to become more than what you are?

ACKNOWLEDGMENTS

I would like to thank all the individuals who read my story while in the draft state and those who helped me make it what it is by providing honest feedback. Without you, this story would not be as awesome as it is!

I would like to acknowledge and give a huge loving thank you to Brittny Mayo, who inspired me to write in the first place. Without Brittny's encouragement, this story may have never been put onto paper.

THE SHOE is a chapter especially dedicated to Brittny Mayo, a beautiful woman and wonderful human being who changed my life forever with her love.

A special thanks goes out to Dylan Hill, who was the very first reader of this story. Dylan read each separate chapter just as quickly as they were written and showed interest in the story, characters, and plot, which reinforced my desire to complete the very first draft.

Thank You! Audrey Co, Brittny Mayo, Adriana Hopkins, and George Adams for taking time out of your busy lives to help me edit this book. Your efforts were crucial to getting some of my phrasing, punctuation, tense, spelling, and grammar correct!

This entire story is dedicated to every human in existence, who understands the idea of love, chooses to right what is wrong, make good what is bad, and give all that they are for the sake of another, without regard for themselves.

INTRODUCTION

love *noun* \'ləv\ as defined by Webster's Dictionary

: a feeling of strong or constant affection for a person
: affection based on admiration, benevolence, or common interests
: attraction that includes sexual desire
: the strong affection felt by people who have a romantic relationship

Since the beginning of recorded history, almost any great deed from the past can be attributed to the concept of love; the love of one's country, the love of God, the love of oneself, and the love of another. One could make the argument that without the feeling or notion which we have labeled "love", humanity would not be where it is today.

Although many people believe they can feel what love is, or have felt what love is, having them try to define that feeling and reduce it to mere words remains a difficult task that always seems to diminish and over simplify the true concept.

It has been spoken that "love" can move mountains, that "love" can conquer all, and that "love" is all we need.

What if that were true?

time *noun* \'tīm\ as defined by Webster's Dictionary

: the measured or measurable period during which an action, process, or condition exists or continues
: a nonspatial continuum that is measured in terms of events which succeed one another from past through present to future
: the point or period when something occurs

Time is a word created by mankind, used to describe the concept of order among events that we, as human beings are aware of and perceive. We categorize these events into three basic sets: events that have already happened, events that are happening, and events that could happen - our past, our present and our future. For most of us, that concept of order will be the only way we will ever perceive and understand the world around us, and our own existence.

For some, that is not so true...

CHAPTER 1 – THE DAY BEFORE

It's Friday, July 11th, 10:30am, and twenty-nine year old Juliandra Lee is interviewing a potential client at the Foundation House, a local drug rehab center where she began working after helping her brother overcome his addiction to cocaine.

Across from her sits a very thin, older man, in his late forties. He's there seeking help because of continuous pressure from his only daughter. The man, Danny Davis, is unable to remain still but is doing his best to answer some questions.

"Mr. Davis, I know this isn't exactly what you want to be doing, but can you tell me how often you use the crystal you get ahold of? Mr. Davis, how many times a week do you use crystal? Once? Twice?"

"I need it a lot, Mrs. Lee. Without the fire, I can't bear to go on each day. It keeps me going."

"How often do you use, Danny?"

"Every day, Mrs. Lee... Every damn day!"

"Okay, Danny, can you to tell me when you first started using drugs?"

"Well, it's been a long time. A long time since I first used something, something to take my worry away."

"Do you think you can remember when?"

"Well, Mrs. Lee, I'll try... I don't know exactly the day but I know I was fifteen. My boys brought me some weed, and it helped me relax. I smoked that for years until I got ahold of some fire. Man, it got me."

"So, you've only tried marijuana and meth?"

"Oh no, I tried lots of 'em, but I didn't know what they were. The boys always had something, always something for me to try. Some of this, some of that. All I knew... I needed it."

Meanwhile, at Rudy Smith's Accounting Services, one town over, thirty-two year old Thomas Lee is sitting in a large office chair, working to resolve a computer issue before his next appointment.

"Damn it! Where the hell are you hiding?" Thomas blurts out, pounding away at a keyboard. "Stupid spyware crap, I'm gonna terminate your ass!"

At that moment, a sprite middle-aged man walks in while combing his hair from left to right with his fingers. He approaches the desk where Thomas is working. "How's it going Thomas?" He asks, "Did you get the systems all fixed up?"

"Oh, I'm workin' on it Rudy. I've found and cleaned up everything except one last process that seems to be hiding from me at the moment, but I'll find it. Should be another thirty to forty-five minutes before this gets done, if all goes well."

"Really, what do you think happened?"

"Well, seems like you might have landed on a website that injected malicious code into your operating system through the web browser. I don't recognize the infection, but that only means I haven't seen it before."

Rudy grabs a file from the desk and starts making his way towards the door before stopping a moment and turning back. "I do a lot of research on the internet and can't afford to have this happen all the time. What can we do to stop this from happening again?"

Thomas, still seated, spins towards Rudy, takes his hands and places them together, fingertip-to-fingertip, just below his lower lip.

"Well, it's like this Rudy. Think of the Internet like you would the world. There are some places in the world you just don't want to be. Places where you might get sick from drinking the water, or mugged because you look out of place, or maybe even kidnapped or killed. If you want to avoid these types of places you should only go where you know it's safe, places you trust. It's easy to take a wrong turn on the web, just like in real life, and end up somewhere you don't want or need to be. All the Internet security software in the world isn't going to help you if you keep visiting places that are hostile and you basically invite the attackers in. It's really a matter of using the Internet in a smart way, rather than being carefree, going from place to place."

Back at the Foundation House, Juliandra sits in a break room eating lunch before a group counseling session with several clients at 1:30pm. The chicken noodle soup she brought in for lunch is steaming as she holds a spoonful in front of her and blows on it. After getting her first taste, Juliandra lowers the spoon back into the bowl, stirs it around while checking her cellphone then stops to compose a text message to Thomas.

SMS: 'I can't wait for this weekend with you. Just us ☺

After hitting 'SEND,' she scoops up more soup as a coworker walks into the room and asks about Danny Davis.

"Juliandra, what's up with Mr. Davis? Is he being accepted to the clinic today? He's telling me that he needs to go and get his fire. What the heck is his fire? What should I do with him?"

"Keep him here until Doctor Fiave arrives." Juliandra replies, "I called him before lunch so he should be here any time. Mr. Davis is addicted to methamphetamines and we need to get him assessed immediately by the doctor. I think he needs a prescription for Desoxyn so we can get him calmed down and gradually wean him off what he's been using.

Juliandra rises out of her seat with the remaining soup to place it on the counter top behind her. As she turns, the bottom of the bowl hits the counter's edge, causing it to drop and break, sending soup everywhere.

"Ahhh!" Juliandra grumbles, "I wanted that soup for later. It's my favorite soup. Well... Gimme a couple of minutes to clean this up Diane, and I'll be out. Keep Mr. Davis occupied for me, please."

A few miles away, Thomas finds himself standing in a checkout line inside Groupard's grocery store, waiting to pay for his lunch before heading to his next appointment. A chicken salad sandwich and small cup of fruit sit in front of him on the mini conveyer belt, moving closer toward Jay, the cashier, who's trying to help an elderly woman figure out the credit card terminal.

Without skipping a beat, like a well-programmed robot, the awkward looking teen hands the woman her receipt, tells her to have a nice day, and then immediately turns to Thomas. "Hi, sir, did you find everything you were looking for today?"

Thomas, unable to help himself and wanting to break up the perpetual repetition the poor kid was clearly trapped in, immediately replies.

"No, I didn't! I came in here to find hot women, and I only saw one in aisle four, and she was already in someone's cart."

The cashier looks stumped for a moment, taken off guard by a very unusual answer to his very standard and well-rehearsed question. Slowly, a smile breaks across his face and he apologizes to Thomas. "I'm sorry sir. I'll let the manager know that we're all out of hot women and that we should order more right away. Your total is $6.79."

Thomas smiles and hands the awkward teen a ten dollar bill. "Well, I guess I'll have to settle for this sandwich for now, but I'm very disappointed, young man."

Still smiling, the cashier places the money in the cash tray and stops to stare at the screen in front of him before handing Thomas his change. Thomas heads out to the parking lot and walks around like a tourist trying to remember where the heck he put his vehicle. After walking down the wrong row of cars, he finally spots his truck one row over, doubles back, and passes a family loading groceries into their minivan. As Thomas walks by, a small girl no older than three, sitting in their shopping cart, smiles and waves to him; Thomas raises his hand and gives a little wave back. Just as he passes the cart by only a few steps, he hears the little girl ask her mom a question. "Mommy, why is that man's nose so big?"

Thomas laughs as he continues towards his truck and mumbles under his breath: *"If adults were that honest to each other, the world would be so different."*

Once inside the truck, Thomas hears a chime from his cell phone and reaches over to the passenger seat to pick it up. Checking the screen, he sees that Juliandra has sent him a text message. A huge smile forms on his face as he quickly replies, *"YES!! ☺,"* before starting the vehicle and getting back on the road.

1:00pm rolls around as Thomas drives into the parking lot of the Clear Pools Company, where he's scheduled to fix some wireless networking issues. He quickly finishes eating his sandwich, gets out of the truck, and wipes crumbs from his clothes before making his way to the front entrance.

Half an hour later, Thomas finds himself stepping down a wooden stairway into a basement at Mainly Law Offices, through an old counterweighted floor opening. After reaching the bottom and walking a few feet towards a wall containing the company's communications equipment, the entrance suddenly slams shut.

"We got another one!" Someone screams from upstairs.

Laughter ensues from above, and with a smirk, Thomas yells back.

"Hah! You got me guys, very funny!"

At this point in the day, Juliandra finds herself in a large meeting room, standing between two men engaged in a heated argument and ready to come to blows. Juliandra calls out to the staff for help, steps back and asks them to calm down and sit in their chairs.

"I know you took it!" one man bellows, "I know you stole my paper! You've been plotting this heist ever since I got to this hellhole. What kind of person are you to take my property?"

"I didn't take anything from you, Asshole" replies the other man. "You're crazy and don't even HAVE a paper!"

"Shut up and just admit it or I'll turn you into paper right now with my fists!"

"Stop it!" Juliandra shouts. "I need for both of you to sit down now! Sit down and we'll find out what happened to your paper, Tony. Just sit down."

Three extra staff members rush into the room at the moment Tony screams and lunges towards the other man, Ryan. "I'll sit down when he gives me my paper back!"

Juliandra continues to back away and waits for the staff to separate the two men as they swing fists with no regard for poor Trevor, a newly hired employee who receives a blow to his nose while trying to intervene. Blood pours from Trevor's nose as the three employees move the arguing pair out of the room and into separate areas of the center. Juliandra lets out a huge sigh, lowers her head, and tells the rest of the group to take a break so she can clean up the mess before continuing their discussions.

After putting on some gloves, Juliandra grabs a bottle labeled 'bleach' from a nearby locked cabinet, begins to spray it over the floor and starts wiping up the blood from Trevor's nose. She mumbles, shaking her head back and forth in disappointment at the utter chaos people can cause. *"Man, if every adult just blurted out what they were thinking all the time, the world would not survive a single day."*

10

Still working in the basement of the law office, Thomas checks the time and notices 4:30pm came fast. He realizes that he needs to work faster if he's going to finish and still have time to lift weights before teaching two taekwondo classes later that evening. Hastily, Thomas begins to wrap things up and then makes his way to the first floor to brief the owner, Samantha Stevens, on the best practices for workstation security.

While at the center filling out paperwork for Danny Davis, who has just been admitted after an examination, Juliandra receives a call. She picks up her cell phone, sees that it's her mother, Regina, and drops her pen before answering.

"Hi Mom, how's your day going?" she asks.

"Juliandra, are you and Thomas coming over this weekend?"

"No, this weekend is ours. We came over last weekend for the barbeque. We've been planning this weekend for the past couple of months but maybe we can come over next weekend."

"Well, you know this weekend I wanted to get my hair done and you promised to do it," Regina replies.

"I will, Mom. I'll do it next weekend, okay? This weekend Thomas and I are going to spend together. It's been so long since we've had a quiet day all to ourselves. I hope you understand."

"Say no more, Juliandra. I'll just look like a fool out on my date Sunday with a nappy head of hair. I understand that your mom, who brought you into this world, and gave you everything, isn't worth the time to help with something as trivial as a haircut."

"Mom! Don't try to guilt me into this! Besides, you don't even have a date! And if you did, who is it?"

"There's a new mechanic down at Frank's Auto and he gave me The Eye a few times."

"New mechanic! Are you for real right now mom? That new mechanic is Frank's dad, and he's just helping out Frank for a couple of weeks."

"Well, he gave me The Eye and I know he wants me, so we're going out Sunday."

"Does he even know he's going out with you? Does he even know you at all, Mom?"

"Well, he will on Sunday, when I show him what…"

Juliandra quickly interrupts. "Mom, that's really gross, and I have to go, but I'll see you next weekend. Okay… Bye mom…"

Back at Mainly Law, Thomas is checking his phone every minute while he waits for the owner to print out a check. Finally, he makes his way out of the building to his truck so he can travel to the YMCA where he exercises and volunteers. As soon as Thomas sits behind the wheel, his cell phone rings. *Juliandra*, he thinks while scrambling to find his smartphone. *Where is that thing?* The ring tone continues to play, until he finds it in one of the pockets of his laptop bag. A quick glance at the caller ID and he answers.

"Hey, man!" Thomas says.

"Hey, it's David," a voice replies.

"What's up?"

"Oh… You know, the daily grind trying to make enough money to pay the bills."

"I hear ya, Man, we gotta do what needs to be done. Are you guys doin' alright?" Thomas asks.

"Yeah we're fine, I'm just calling to give you a heads up that Ray has been drinking a lot again, and Joanne is talking about leaving him."

"Here we go again! You know what? That's it David. One of two things is gonna happen; either we have some kind of intervention to get Ray some help, or I'm gonna write him off. I've got zero tolerance for that crap nowadays."

"I know man. I just wanted to let you know that most likely Joanne's gonna leave him if he doesn't stop drinking. If she leaves him, he'll just drink more, and then his liver is shot."

"Why do people do this?! You know, after Mom and Dad got divorced when we were kids and you got sent away to live with Dad in Maine, I was surrounded by people who drank every hour of the day, did drugs and robbed everyone. It's shocking that I didn't take up drinking or drugs or stealing."

"You're preaching to the choir, Man. I mean, I did a little drinking but never really got into it like Ray. I don't know man, I think some people just need help to get them to relax or maybe forget about life."

"Well, I don't want to forget about life at all. We lost Dad to cancer, Mom died a week later from hepatitis, you almost died after falling from that roof last year, and I nearly died when I wrecked Tim's motorcycle. Life seems pretty damn important to me."

"Ray's gonna be next if his drinking doesn't stop soon. His liver can't hold out much longer. He and Joanne are coming back from some campground Monday."

"Perfect. We're having an intervention with him Monday then. You and I are gonna go over there and get him some help. We need to get him enrolled in AA. There's one in Ellsworth and we're going whether he likes it or not. I'm sick of losing my family members."

"Sounds like a plan to me. I'll take off work, and we can meet at his house first thing."

"Alright, Monday, first thing. I have a few appointments to change, but I'll be there and, I swear, if I've gotta tie that man up and drag his ass to get some help, I will. Can you chat with Joanne and let her know what we're gonna do?"

"I'll call her right now and let her in on the plan. Just relax this weekend and try to enjoy Saturday with Juliandra. When Monday comes, we'll get Ray to Ellsworth. I'm gonna call the AA office out there also and make sure they know we're hopefully coming out."

"Thanks man. Let me know if anything changes or comes up."

"10-4, talk to ya later."

"Alright, later."

Thomas ends the call and tosses his phone into the passenger seat, then hits the steering wheel in anger. "What is wrong with people?!" he yells out. "Ahhh!"

After a brief pause, Thomas grabs his keys, starts the truck, and proceeds to the YMCA. Once he gets there, he goes to the locker room where he tries to quickly change before having to witness the usual immodest behavior of the naked older generation. Unfortunately, he ends up being scarred, once again, when he's forced to watch a 70-year-old man apply medicated powder to his groin. Thomas picks up his pace and pretends not to notice the old guy, who has now asked him about a basketball game while slapping powder on his genitals, two feet from his face. He explains that he really isn't into basketball then quickly rushes out and down a stairway leading to the weight room. After walking through the gym entrance, Thomas mumbles, "Finally!" He sees three friends who are already working out and makes his way towards them.

"What's up, Losers?" Thomas says as he walks passed them on the way to an elliptical machine. His friend, Richard, turns towards him, flexes his right arm, and replies, "Bullet proof is what's up, Homo. You know you want this but can't have it!"

Thomas and his other two friends, Terry and Jeff, start laughing and carry on. A few minutes later, Thomas finds himself doing squats, grunting loudly, holding a barbell loaded with 365 pounds on his back. Terry is spotting him, spewing out his typical words of encouragement. "Come on, drive it up, Loser! My little sister could do twice this weight and not cry about it."

One last, loud grunt and Thomas finally drives the weight upward and places the barbell onto the safety hooks. He wipes the sweat from his forehead and peers over at Richard who's staring at himself in a mirror, flexing. Thomas goes out of his way to walk over to where Richard is standing and stops to stand right next to him. "Why don't you just go rub one out and get it over with, Man? You love yourself way too much."

Richard turns to Thomas. "That's right! But I'm too sexy for just myself, so I've gotta share with the ladies."

"You mean with the other guys in the sauna? Ohh! Does it hurt? Hah!"

"Only when you look at me during!"

"Well then, on that note, I will leave you alone with your fantasies, sir. Please stay out of society for a while so we all can feel safer. I have to go. See you guys tomorrow. Time for my class... Later!"

Another stop in the locker room and Thomas finds himself again shaking his head, as the older generation seems to have no problem with parading around unclothed talking about politics and money. He quickly swaps his gym shorts for the long white pants that make up the lower half of his taekwondo uniform then rushes out the door to a lower level studio where he teaches.

Meanwhile, Juliandra left the center and was on her way to Revel High School, where she works with girls through the Big Brothers Big Sisters program. Today, she had a small group of five girls scheduled to play basketball and discuss teamwork. Juliandra arrived and got all the girls to circle up. Without any hesitation, she begins.

"OK, my lovely ladies, today we learn more about teamwork. I've got the power to take five young women to see Wyatt Keith's next concert at the Civic Center. And I'm thinking that I want to take five girls who can work as a team."

"Wyatt Keith!" one of the girls yells out. "Are you serious? That man's gonna be the father of my children. Awww!! I love 'Don't Stop My Love,' that's my favorite song."

The girl starts to sing the lyrics while swaying back and forth.

"I'm gonna make it, then break it, and get me some... I'm gonna check it, then wreck it, and have me one... It could be tonight... Yeahhhh! It could your night... Yeahhhh! Don't! Stop my love, don't! Stop my love..."

"Oh really," Juliandra says, "I believe you need to meet him first, don't ya think? So, here's the deal ladies, you need to keep this basketball in the air for ninety seconds, like a volleyball, without letting it hit the ground. And... all of you have to be involved. None of you can hit it twice in a row. If it falls, you start over until you reach ninety seconds."

"Ahh, that'll be easy Mrs. Lee," one girl says.

"No problem, let's do this," says another.

Juliandra immediately throws the ball in the air and yells, "Ready go!" All of the girls run towards it at the same time, smashing into each other like a terrible multi-car pileup on the highway. Juliandra laughs, tells them to work out a plan, and walks over to the bleachers to watch.

"This is where you all must collaborate as a team," she calls out.

The girls gather together and begin to argue about the order in which they'll hit the ball upward.

Back at the YMCA, Thomas is tying on his black belt in a basement level studio, as kids begin to fill the room, asking questions.

"When can I test for my green tip Mr. Lee?" asks a nine-year-old boy named Steven. "I want my tip so bad, and everyone else is a higher rank than me."

Thomas looks at Steven and smiles. "It's not about your tip or your belt; it's about who you are, what you know, and how you act."

"I know Mr. Lee, but I want the tip and then I want my green belt too, everyone else has theirs."

"Soon, Steven, soon... And no, everyone else doesn't have theirs, and those that do have them, had to earn it. Be patient and re-tie your belt the correct way because it's not right."

"Okay..."

"Okay?" Thomas says.

"I mean, Yes, sir..."

"Alright, let's go and get ready to line up."

Inside the gym over at Revel High School, five teenage girls are working hard as a team to keep a basketball in the air for ninety seconds. After failing 7 times already, it seems they may have gotten into teamwork mode on the eighth attempt and are very close to reaching a full minute. The group had finally settled on remaining in a circle pattern and swatting the ball upward and over to the person standing to their right, so that it would simply go around to each of them over and over.

Juliandra is looking at a stopwatch in her right hand while it counts up. Seventy seconds, eighty seconds and then ninety seconds go by. She just smiles, says nothing, and lets them continue. The timer reaches one hundred and twenty seconds

18

and Juliandra can hardly contain herself while the girls keep the ball bouncing in the air. The timer reaches one hundred and eighty three seconds before the ball escapes the group and falls to the ground. All of the girls look over at Juliandra, who's clapping her hands, and ask, "How long this time?"

Juliandra yells out, "Three minutes!! You guys got it and did it for double the time! Guess where you're all going?"

The girls scream out with joy, jumping up and down while Juliandra gets up from the bleachers and walks towards them.

"Now, who wants to play some basketball?" she asks.

Thomas's youth class has ended at the YMCA and now he's part way through the Adult class, demonstrating a practical use for an exercise they did during the beginning warm-up called a 'hip heist.' Thomas is on the ground with a student who's acting as an attacker that has tackled him to the floor. He explains that if you get a chance it's possible to raise your hip with one leg and one arm then kick towards your attacker with the other leg to gain enough space to try and stand up.

Thomas raises his hip off the floor, as explained, and proceeds to push away the student with his right foot. As soon as Thomas creates some space between him and the student he quickly stands up and delivers a mock blow to the students face with his right knee. He notes afterwards that circumstances vary so much, that it's impossible to teach exact defense for every situation, therefore, it's up to them to practice the basics and improvise on the fly.

"Whatever you do, try not to end up on the ground in the first place; but if you do, get up as soon as you can. Now, everyone grab a partner and practice."

19

8:00pm hits and Juliandra lets her group know that the game of half court they're playing will be the last for the evening. After the final shot's made, she tells them that it's time to get changed and head home. Before leaving the court, each girl attempts to make one last shot from the three-point line, a tradition started by Juliandra when they first started playing. Three of the five girls make it in before Juliandra steps up to take her turn. She grabs the ball, spins around with her back to the hoop and tosses the ball over her head. It goes in without hitting the rim and makes that sought after infamous swoosh sound. Juliandra turns with a surprised look on her face then bows to all the girls clapping loudly as they make their way to the locker room entrance.

Over at the YMCA, Thomas is finishing up, thinking to himself, home would be a good place to be right now. He rushes his movements and makes his way out of the building saying good night to everyone on the way. Thomas hops into his truck and rushes home to find Juliandra waiting for him on the living room couch. He plops down beside her and they both let out a big sigh.

"We made it," Thomas says. "We made it to the weekend."

"Thank God," Juliandra replies. "Although, I did make an awesome shot today from the three point line. I shot without even looking and, by some miracle, the ball went in. It was awesome!"

"That was no miracle baby. That was your dad looking out for you. He knows you can't play, so he was trying to help you out."

"Whatever! I made that shot all by myself."

"I know you did, and I think you could do it again, no problem. Care to bet on it?"

"No, you know I don't bet on things. Maybe if you're lucky and we play, I will bless you with my graceful skill; then you'll see the miracle shot."

"Does your brother still play or does he just mess around like at the barbeque last weekend? I'd ask him, but I don't think he likes me much at all. In fact, he seems to hate me."

"Brighten doesn't hate you."

"Yeah, he does. He acts juvenile when I'm around and makes awful comments. It's pretty much hatred."

"We've gone over this a bunch of times Thomas. Brighten hates what you represent, not you."

"What's the difference? Hate is hate. And what stinks is that he sucks me in to that crap and I just make stupid comments right back."

"Give Brighten some time to accept you; he's a very proud person and just doesn't like the fact that I'm married to someone who's white."

"It's been four years! How much time does it take? I don't hate him, although, he is kind of an ass all the time. I've tried to get him to do things with me, but he just doesn't wanna even try."

"Look; to him, you and I shouldn't be; and he hates the fact that a black woman would even choose to be with a white man. That's just how it is, and nothing but Brighten can change that. He's gotta get over it and move on, not you."

"Well, I wish the guy would just talk to me and see what kind of person I am, that's all. He just makes his usual smart-ass comments and tells me how much I suck. It's like we're in fifth grade or something. What about your dad? Do you think your dad would've accepted me?"

"If my dad was alive, I think you'd be dead."

"What?"

With a little chuckle, Juliandra says, "I'm just kidding, my father was a very forgiving person, and I believe he would've only shot you in the leg or something, so you wouldn't have died."

"Great!" Thomas blurts out while getting up to grab a drink of water. "You could be married to a gimpy white guy with a bum leg."

"Yeah, but you know, I'd still love that poor gimpy white guy with the bum leg. I would wait for you to take your little gimpy steps while we went grocery shopping. Hey, that would actually work well I think. You could gimp around with the shopping cart while I cruised everywhere to get things. Hmmmm"

"Oh, really? Well, I guess Gimpy's gonna have to show you what's up." Thomas leans over Juliandra and puts his arms around her waist, squats down, lifts her up from the couch while she giggles and screams out, "Stop Gimpy stop!"

He puts her over his right shoulder and takes her into the bedroom. As they get close to the bed Thomas leans forward, drops her onto the mattress and looks down at her. He takes a step back, reaches for the center of his shirt, and rips it open, causing several small white buttons to shoot all over the room.

One bounces off the wall and another hits the nightstand before landing on the floor.

Thomas looks right at Juliandra with a smirk. "Gimpy said it's on now!"

Juliandra bursts into laughter. "This isn't romantic at all. It's a comedy show."

Thomas removes his shirt and walks over to the bathroom. "I'll be back!" he says, just before closing the door.

Juliandra, still wiping tears of laughter from her eyes, starts to change her clothes. Suddenly, Thomas burst out of the bathroom with a serious look on his face.

"How am I so lucky to be married to you?" he says. "You accept me for who I am, and always treat me good. How is it that someone so beautiful could be with me? Do you know how much I love you?"

Juliandra's expression changes while only part way through putting on her nightgown.

"Show me, Thomas, show me how much you love me."

Thomas walks over and pulls her close. He reaches out to caress her left cheek, and begins to kiss her passionately.

CHAPTER 2 - THE MORNING

The warmth and brightness of the sun's rays shining through a bedroom window eventually triggers Thomas to open his eyes. Glancing at an old style analog clock on the bedroom wall becomes delusive as Thomas remembers how much he hates trying to determine the time from those types of clocks. It always seems to takes his brain way too long to convert what he sees into a number he understands.

After reaching for his cell phone lying on the nightstand he looks with a feeling of comfort when the familiar digits on the screen come in to view. 8:36am, Saturday, July 12th. A quick sigh of relief, and he turns to see the morning's light reflecting from Juliandra's smooth skin. She's beginning to wake and her lips slowly form a smile as he gently moves closer and begins kissing her neck repeatedly. A few seconds go by before he stops and whispers into her ear.

"Hey, hey... I need your help with something. I think someone slipped me one of those pills last night."

Juliandra shifts her head slightly towards him without opening her eyes and asks. "What pills? What the heck are you talking about?"

"You know, one of those pills that makes your... umm... your thingy become supersized. I need your help because I hear it's bad to let 'em stay that way, and I have to use it or I could be injured or something."

Juliandra starts to laugh when Thomas begins kissing her neck with loud lip smacking sounds. The mood of humor soon changes to that of romance as the sound of giggles transforms to moans, and the comforter gets pulled up and over their bodies.

The morning light brightens, and for a while, the two remain in bed holding each other closely, sharing laughs about past mistakes.

"Christmas, 1998," Juliandra says.

"Why? What mistake did you make that year?"

"Well… When I was thirteen, I was really into Brenda Braxton. I mean I just loved all her songs. I loved how she looked because she was such a beautiful black woman. And, I loved what she represented, an independent female who could do just anything. She was glamorous, talented, and could sang!"

"Huhh" Thomas replies, "I liked a couple of her songs back in the day. Well, I still like 'em today actually."

"Me too, but back then, I really wanted to be just like her. So, I would try and sing along to her songs when I heard them, and I would try to look glamorous while doing it. I had my poses down and everything!"

"Hah, I bet you were pretty good. Care to demonstrate some of those poses?"

"Not a chance! I was thirteen. I'm not doin' them now."

"Come on… Just a couple."

"Anyways… Like I was saying, I really wanted to be like her, so I kept asking my mom for a dress like the one Brenda had on at the 1997 Music Awards Show. It was a beautiful two tone dress with white in the front and brown down each side. I think I asked her a hundred times for it."

Thomas chuckles a bit "Did she smack you for asking too much? Oh, I can see her pulling off one those shoes and waving it around in the air. 'Girl, you better get to your room and stop asking me about that damn dress!'"

"Ha ha, funny. No! She didn't hit me for asking, but she did smack me straight plenty of other times. Nah, she just kept tellin' me that if it comes, it comes, and if it don't, it don't, and that's that. And a few times, she would say 'Ask your father!' and I would just tell her that dad wasn't home yet."

"Was he working or something?"

"Yeah… He was working extra hours for two months and we only got to see him for a few minutes before bed that whole time."

"Well, what the heck was your mistake? I'm sure you got wacked by a shoe for something."

"Let me finish my story, boy. So, Christmas came around and that morning I ran out into the living room. All I wanted to do was find my present and see what it was."

"Present? Just one? You only got one thing?"

"Uh huh, did I not mention how poor we were? Brighten got one thing and I got one thing and we were damn lucky to have whatever we got, even if we didn't like it."

"Wow, we were poor too, but I think my mom took our stuff apart and wrapped the separate pieces to make it look like we had a bunch of presents. I remember opening stuff up and low and behold it all created one toy. I thought it was genius."

"Your momma was a smart cookie. We just got the one and that Christmas I waited for Brighten to open up his present so I could open mine. I just couldn't wait to get the wrapping off."

"Wait, what did Brighten get? Do you remember?"

"Oh yeah, I remember every detail of that morning. Brighten was so happy when he tore off the newspaper to find a brand new basketball. He would not stop dribbling that ball all day and I'm pretty sure he got a whooping later for dribbling in the house."

"He got a basketball that year?"

"Yup"

"So, that basketball wouldn't happen to be one of the older leather looking ones?"

"Yup, he still has it. It doesn't hold air well anymore but he keeps it around for some reason."

"Ahhh... Go on."

"Well, for a few seconds, I was so happy for Brighten that I forgot about my gift. I was watching him smile, bouncing it and acting like he was a pro player. As soon as dad yelled at him to stop, I remembered the present in my hands. Mom told me to open it up and when I did, I started jumping up and down. It was a dress that looked just like the one Brenda Braxton had on. It wasn't exactly the same, but it was damn close. I loved it. I kissed mom then ran over to my dad and kissed him. And, I said thank you twenty times while prancing around holding it in front of me."

"Hmm, that sounds like a happily ever after moment to me. So, why did you get smacked?"

"I told you, I didn't get smacked fool. I loved that dress so much I wore it everywhere and all the time. Mom had to pry it off me in order to wash it, and as soon as she did I had it on again. One day, I was outside playing with my friend Arial and we were taking turns riding an old bicycle up and down the driveway. On one of my turns, the lower part of the dress got caught in the chain, by the pedals and it ripped."

"I knew it! And Regina came out, and beat you with her shoe for ripping your dress! I knew you got a smack down!"

"Wrong again. Mom came out, and saw me crying about the dress. It was ripped pretty bad too. She just told me to go inside and change so she could try to fix it. I did. I went in, put on different clothes and in a little while, forgot all about the dress. I just kept playing outside and mom never said another word about it to me."

"What the heck man? Someone better be gettin' smacked soon in this story."

"I never said anyone got smacked. A couple days later, I overheard my parents talking about not being able to pay the electric bill, and dad was mad. He told my mom that he worked so much; he didn't feel like he was part of the family anymore. He said he was gone all day and never got to see us grow up. I listened to them talk for a long time until they caught me and made me go to bed, but I found out that the reason dad was working so much was to make up for the money they spent on my dress and Brighten's basketball. My mistake sir... was asking for that dress. I would never have asked for it, if I had understood how much it cost them to get for me. I would've gladly traded it for the extra time to spend with my dad. Just to have him home instead of working all the time. And you know what? I never asked for anything else after that."

"Holy cow girl! That's deep... You win this one. I totally give up because I've got nothing on that mistake. I did **not** see that coming. I really thought it was gonna be a funny story."

"Well Brighten did get a whoopin'; that was pretty funny."

"Hah! That's right, he did and yes, that's funny with no end to it. Now, whenever he starts flappin' to me, all I'm gonna do is picture your mom beating him with a shoe."

After a few more laughs, the two decide to get up and share some hot tea in the kitchen while telling one another silly unknown facts about themselves.

"No seriously, I have moves. You've seen my moves," Thomas says.

"Oh you've got moves alright." Juliandra replies, "You do have some kind of moves. Not sure what to call 'em but they're moves I suppose."

"Well, despite how great I can dance at home, I tend to freeze out in public. I just can't get myself to move in public. It's like someone flips a switch and I forget how to move my body."

"Oh, is that what it is? I thought it was more like you just didn't do your moves because it was too embarrassing."

"No way! I got awesome moves, I just freeze in public."

"Oh, I hear ya. Did I ever tell you that when I was seven years old, I told my mom that I was going to be a pole dancer?"

Thomas bursts into laughter and spits the tea he's sipping out onto the kitchen table. "Say what?"

"Oh my god, it was so funny. I saw a show on TV where this girl was pole dancing and I thought it was like gymnastics or something, I was really impressed at how this lady was able to spin around and hang off the pole."

"What kind of shows were you watching as a child?"

"I don't remember what it was. It could have been a movie or something but I told my mom that I was gonna become a pole dancer, and she looked at me like I had gone insane. I remember that look like it was yesterday; her eyes got all wide and her eyebrows went up really high. She was cooking on the stove and dropped a spoon onto the counter. She just said 'Oh, really Juliandra?' and I told her that I had just seen someone pole dancing on TV and that it was so cool, like gymnastics. After I got done explaining all about it and why I was going to be the best pole dancer ever, she laughed and laughed. I don't think I'd ever seen my mom laugh so much before. When she couldn't laugh anymore, she told me what pole dancing was really all about, the nice version mind you, and I was so embarrassed."

"I just can't win with you, can I? Every single story I have, you have one better. I could say like... Umm, hey, I flew to the moon yesterday and you would be all like... Well, I did that when I was six and then I went to Jupiter for a week. One of these days I'm gonna have a better story and win."

"Keep trying boy; I have some good stories left yet."

It's now 9:16am and Juliandra offers to make breakfast if Thomas agrees to dance with her a few moments while singing lyrics from one of her favorite songs. He immediately springs to his feet doing his best impression of a proper dancing posture, reaches out for Juliandra's hand, pulls her close and stares into her eyes with a slight squint, one eye brow raised and lightly puckered lips. He takes one step backwards and with a serious face, begins to yell out the words to a well-known rap song about grinding on the dance floor. He then quickly spins around and begins to push his hind end towards her bobbing it up and down while singing the chorus line.

Juliandra laughingly yells out: "Not that song! My other favorite song!"

Thomas spins back around with a big smile, gives her a hug and reaches for her right hand. He leads her in a slow romantic sway, singing in a quiet soothing tone. He knew the song she wanted to hear and had memorized all the lyrics to serenade her at the right moments. Even though he can't really sing, Juliandra still loves hearing his voice and just closes her eyes while Thomas does his best.

After dancing a short while and a kiss to seal the deal, they break free and Juliandra starts gathering everything needed to make breakfast for the two of them. Thomas walks over to the trash and proceeds to take it outside to the larger cans in front of the house. On his way back he stops at a pile of mail on the sofa table near the front door and takes a quick glimpse at each envelope, but finds nothing of interest.

Unimpressed, Thomas walks back into the kitchen where he makes eye contact with Juliandra and smiles. At the same time he catches a glimpse of the microwave clock, which shows the time of 9:36am. Then he notices a glass on the counter suddenly burst into pieces and scatter throughout the kitchen. The window Juliandra is standing by shatters and glass seems to fly everywhere while a magnetic clip, holding their grocery list on the refrigerator, explodes allowing the paper to fall.

Thomas turns his head back to look at Juliandra and yells out: "What the hell!" Juliandra spins around with a look of fear and shock, both hands on the side of her face. Soon, her look changes from fear to confusion and then to agony as she suddenly drops to the floor in pain.

Screaming out her name, Thomas runs over to grab and pull Juliandra into the living room. He drops to his knees and holds her in his arms. Frantically, he starts to check all over her body for wounds while she lies on the floor barely able to speak and struggling to breathe. Blood pools outward as her breath becomes more and more shallow. Thomas keeps pressing where he thinks it's coming from, but he's dumbfounded, emotionally charged, and can't think straight as the red continues to flow.

Her life is fading quickly and with both arms, Thomas embraces Juliandra.

"No! No! No!" He yells out.

Slowly, he leans away to see her face and looks into her eyes as she reaches for him. Juliandra's arms drop quickly, as if a switch had been flipped, turning off her ability to move. Looking up at him, her shallow breath turns to panting as she attempts to speak. "My life... Thomas, I... love... yhhh"

Absolutely nothing in the universe could possibly distract his gaze, and in this moment, Thomas feels a sharp pain around his heart. It was a pain so terrible, like someone cutting it from his chest with a dull knife. Tears uncontrollably and rapidly flow and fall from his eyes.

"I love you Juliandra." He cries. "Don't leave me!"

Then with every ounce of thought, intent, and being, he expels any trace of air left in his lungs as he screams out her name one last time, "**JULIANDRA!**"

For a split second, time seems to pause. No more sound exists, no more motion, no more pain; only the vision of Juliandra's face and a single tear, which had fallen from her eye, frozen in place. Thomas's heart, which was healthy and strong, stops beating at the same moment Juliandra slips away. A sudden brightness that fades to black and his body slowly collapses backward onto the floor beside her.

Silence...

No voices. No wind. No heart beats. No life as darkness fills the room and existence ceases to be.

CHAPTER 3 - THE RECOVERY

Nothingness encompasses all, until a stinging pain shoots through the darkness accompanied by a flash of light. Soon, another flash, and the sting is stronger. Pain comes again, and another brief moment of light which fades away just as before. A final flash brings with it more hurt than all the rest, but the light does not fade this time. A small amount remains. It's steady, shaped like a small circle and appears to be turning. Thomas begins to focus on it as the noise of sirens and the chatter of people talking become louder and louder until the full volume of the world slams into him.

"We have a pulse! I'm reading a pulse!" Shouts an EMT.

"It's stable; let's get him in the ambulance! I think we got here just in time to save him. Who knows how long he was gone."

Thomas barely opens his eyes as he regains consciousness, just a bit at first, only enough to allow a thin line of brightness in. The ambulance is moving fast, and after a few minutes Thomas finally starts to look around but is dazed, confused, and immediately begins to cry uncontrollably. As the memories of this morning's tragedy start to flood back, he suddenly understands the reason for his tears and why he can't stop them. His head hurts worse than any migraine he's ever had, and his body feels heavy and hard to move.

The people surrounding him are asking questions, but Thomas is unable to respond and stops trying. He remains still, blinking away the buildup of moisture causing his vision to blur every few seconds. Every bump in the road causes a pulse of pain to shoot through his head and the light above hurts, so he looks to the side. Soon, they arrive in front of a hospital's emergency room entrance and the EMTs rush him in.

The hand off is made to the hospital's ER staff while the ambulance crew updates them on Thomas's vitals. Nurses quickly move Thomas into an open room and connect him to a cardiac monitor. After a couple of hours and no sign of trouble, he's moved again to a standard room for observation where he begins to slowly show signs of awareness and starts quietly crying out.

"Where's Juliandra? Where is Juliandra?" he says.

A nurse named Rachel approaches.

"I don't know where Juliandra is sir. We'll find out for you alright. Now, try and relax. Just lie back and relax."

His vision is blurry, but he can make out the silhouettes that seem to be talking to each other.

"Jim, I don't know who he is, but the EMTs tell me that he could've been gone for several minutes before they revived him. They don't know how long he was without a heartbeat and who knows what kind of brain damage has occurred."

"Alright, alright... Let's keep him under observation and wait for the authorities to tell us what's happened. We need to pull his medical records right away. See if you can get his name, social, or something."

"Hey!" Thomas yells out. "My name is Thomas Lee! Thomas Lee! Where's my wife, Juliandra?"

The doctor walks over, close to him, and calls a nurse to the room.

"Rachel, can you please pull up any records we have for a Thomas Lee, right away?" He leans over Thomas, looking into his eyes.

"Thomas, can you understand me?"

"Yes," Thomas replies.

"Listen, can you tell me if you have any medical issues with your heart?"

"No," Thomas says, "Nothing."

"Thomas, did you take anything before this happened? Any medications, drugs, or alcohol? Anything you can remember?"

"No... Nothing." he replies, frustrated. "My wife, she's gone. Juliandra's gone."

"We're still waiting for the authorities, Thomas. Try to relax. We'll find out where she is, just relax."

Thomas looks at the buzzing fluorescent lights on the ceiling and wipes away the tears that continue to build up. He can't seem to stop them, and it takes several minutes to control the outbursts of emotion that have become dominant and refuse to subside.

A short while later he finds himself being questioned by two officers investigating the situation. They're trying to get answers about the day's events.

"I was just standing there and she fell to the ground. I didn't know what was happening and I pulled her away and kept pulling her. I couldn't save her. It happened in the blink of an eye. I blacked out after that. I just don't know what happened." Thomas explains.

Juliandra's brother and mom arrive while the two men are listening to his description of what happened. Regina is in tears, while Brighten seems filled with anger as they approach.

"Where is my daughter?" Regina asks. "Where's Juliandra?"

One of the officers explains that Juliandra did not survive and her body was taken for an autopsy to determine the exact cause of death. He also tells her that from what they could see, she had been shot three times. Regina nearly drops to the floor crying, but Brighten reacts quickly, reaches out and is able to hold her up.

"Ms. Jones, we'll have the results soon and will inform you as we know more. We'll be using every resource at our disposal to find whoever did this."

Brighten immediately speaks out in anger. "Was it Thomas? Was it him? Did he do it?"

"No, Mr. Jones, as far as we can tell, Thomas is not a suspect. We don't believe he could have done this. Everything he's told us seems to check out and until we can prove otherwise, we must assume he's innocent. The shots came from outside the home and according to their neighbor, a mister Holland Grant, both Juliandra and Thomas were inside at the time."

Thomas calls for Brighten to come near the bed. "Brighten, I swear to you, I don't know what happen. Juliandra was in the kitchen and then she…." Unable to finish his sentence, Thomas begins to cry.

Brighten looks down at Thomas with bloodshot eyes and a lifetime of rage.

"You better hope you're not involved, Thomas, or I swear, I will skin your white ass and leave you to die."

Regina quickly embraces Thomas and shouts, "Enough! I want to see my son-in-law alone, right now! Brighten, he didn't do it. Please, wait outside."

One of the officers hands Thomas a card and explains that he will need to make a formal statement as soon as possible. Brighten and the two men leave the room, but remain outside after closing the door. Regina, still embracing Thomas and in tears, asks him to explain.

"Thomas, please tell me what happened to Juliandra. Oh, my Juliandra... Thomas, what's going on?"

"I don't know Regina. We had a wonderful night and were looking forward to today, just the two of us together. We danced in the kitchen, I took the trash outside and when I went back in she was standing there. I saw her.... I saw her fall to the floor in agony. Oh my God... Juliandra's gone!"

Regina and Thomas remain in the room until the doctor comes back and asks everyone, including the officers, to leave.

"Thomas must be left to rest now. We have him under observation and he needs to relax so we can make sure his vitals remain stable. You can see him again tomorrow. Okay."

The doctor walks over to Thomas.

"Mr. Lee, I know all of this is very traumatic but, I have a job to do and that job is to keep you alive and healthy. Please try to keep yourself calm. I promise that I'll do whatever it takes to help you. I can't however give you any medication to help you sleep at this point because we're unsure what the cause of your cardiac event was. Please, try to rest."

"Alright," Thomas replies, "Alright."

Thomas is suddenly left to his own thoughts and the ambient noises of the monitoring equipment surrounding him. The morning plays out over and over in his head as he turns from one side of the bed to the other. The tears won't stop as he becomes more and more upset. He feels responsible.

"I couldn't save her! I couldn't save her!" He cries out, sweat pouring down his face.

Nurse Rachel pops in and rushes over.

"Mr. Lee, you have to relax, your heart rate is too high; we need to get it down."

"I can't relax, I lost my wife. I couldn't save her."

Rachel calls for the doctor and waits for his arrival.

"Doctor, we have to do something with Mr. Lee; he can't calm down and his adrenaline levels are causing his heart rate to stay high."

The doctor turns a page in a file folder he is holding. "I just finished looking through his records and I see nothing regarding any medical conditions at all. I'm going to prescribe a single .5mg dose of Ativan to help him get through tonight. Please, get it to him as soon as you can and watch his vitals closely."

"Yes, Doctor, I'm on it."

Moments later, Nurse Rachel returns to Thomas's room with the prescribed medication and what she considers good news for Thomas.

"Mr. Lee, I'm going to give you a small dose of something called Ativan, to help you sleep. The doctor looked at your records and believes you should be fine to have it."

Thomas nods his head. "I hate medications," he says, "but I'll try anything right now."

"It'll just take me a few seconds to get this ready," Nurse Rachel explains.

Thomas sits up. "How long does it take nurse? How long till it helps?"

"Oh, you can lie back Mr. Lee. This will go right through your IV. You don't have to take it orally. Some of the medications can take hours to work when taken orally. This should be almost immediate."

"Ahh"

"Alright, here we go. Try to relax your mind. Your brain can help the process or fight it; it's very powerful. "

"I'll try, thank you."

"We're done," Nurse Rachel says. "Just relax. I'm going to turn off the room light now to help you sleep."

Instantly, the appearance of the room alters with the sound of the light switch changing position. Thomas stares upward trying to calm his mind, but a continuous stream of thoughts reminding him of reality keeps relaxation at bay. He finds himself drawn to the light emitted by each piece of equipment placed around the bed, and her face is all he can think of; her beautiful smile, her perfect lips, and her soft brown skin as he caresses it. Eventually, the small lights keeping his attention start to fade, ambient noise begins to quiet, and nothingness becomes everything.

CHAPTER 4 - THE REPEATING

A strong sensation of warmth causes Thomas to raise his arm and cover his face. *Where?* He wonders. *Where are the sounds I fell asleep to? Where are those noises that I tried so desperately to ignore?* He doesn't want to open his eyes and see that damn hospital room again. It was just too much, so Thomas remains still, trying not moving at all. *What is this heat on my face?* He keeps thinking. *Is someone shining a light at me on purpose?* The temperature seemed to be increasing and the room was clearly becoming brighter. Finally, his eyes open and he sits up, extending his arms back. *OH, My God, what a nightmare.*

Thomas looks around until a familiar clock on the wall catches his attention and draws him into full consciousness. *Man... I hate those clocks,* he thinks. After rubbing his eyes he lies back, turns to his side and reaches for a cell phone beside the bed. The screen shows 8:37am. *Fantastic! In my nightmare it was 8:36.*

Everything seems normal as he reaches for Juliandra and pulls her close. The embrace is a little more snug than usual; as if he wants to make sure her body is really there. Gently, he caresses her cheek then slowly runs his hand down her arm as he begins to whisper.

"Hey, I need your help with something. I think someone slipped me one of those..." His words suddenly stop as a strong sense of déjà vu overwhelms his mind.

Juliandra turns slightly. "Those what? What the heck are you talking about?"

Déjà vu again? He thinks. *Nah, she always says something like that.*

"Oh, nothing, I had a joke and forgot how it went. You know, I think we should just go at it until we can't anymore."

Juliandra turns to face him and replies with a smirk, "Go at what? Just what is it that we would be going at until we can't anymore?"

"You know what I'm talkin' about. Remember that article in Men's Health magazine? The one that said men need to basically do it all the time to prevent prostate cancer."

He begins to loudly kiss Juliandra all over her face.

"My health is at risk woman and you must save me!"

The humorous sounds and giggles slowly change to a softer more romantic tone when the two pull the comforter up and over their bodies. As the morning progresses they remain in bed holding each other and talking.

"It was so real!" Thomas says. "So real. You'd been shot and I couldn't do anything to save you, I lost you."

"I'm right here." Juliandra replies. "You haven't lost me at all. Besides, could you have made love to a ghost? I mean, you must have realized I was real during the entire thirty seconds of romantic love making, right?"

"Thirty seconds! I lasted at least ninety seconds! I think you need to check your clock girl! I mean I don't think you could handle much more than that."

Both laugh for a bit before discussing what they might do during the day, but each time an idea is brought up, Thomas feels as if they've already talked about it. He then tries to change the conversation to a subject that doesn't seem familiar.

"Hey, remember last weekend when we were at your mother's for the barbeque? After we left I asked about your conversation with Carol. You mentioned it was deep, and I never got a chance to hear what you guys were discussing."

"I did? Yeah, I guess it was pretty deep. She was really interested in my past. Dating and boyfriends, stuff like that."

"Ahh, the 'ex' discussion. Did you tell her about Craig?"

"I did actually; I don't know why, but I told her all about him."

"That must be a female thing because none of the guys in my little world tend to ask or even bring up past girlfriends. It's kinda like the women in their lives don't even exist. Come to think of it, I never hear much of anything about current or past girlfriends from the guys. Except Richard; he's always talking about his ex-girlfriend, who was supposedly really hot and how he should bang her again."

"That's nice. How romantic... Not! Richard is something else."

"Yeah, he is. Pretty hilarious sometimes to. So, how detailed did you get?"

"Umm, not too much, just a bit about how we got together, how he affected Brighten, and how the whole experience helped me find you. We didn't talk about sex if that's what you're driving at."

"No sex talk! I'm amazed. It seems like women always talk about sex. I mean, come on, that's where all the measurements come up, right? Don't you guys carry stat sheets around with measurements and times?"

"Wow, that would just be nasty. But you know what, that's not a bad idea."

"You should, I know all the guys do. Heck, I have my sheet around here somewhere." Thomas starts looking around, pretending to hunt for an imaginary paper.

Juliandra smiles and nudges Thomas. "So you've got a sheet do you? Got my measurements on it? I'm curious; do you put my time on there or your time?"

"Just kidding, just kidding! No sheets exists. Let's just all forget about times and sheets. There's no times written anywhere. What is time anyway? Who really cares about silly things like time?"

"Yeah, that's what I thought."

Thomas reaches over and hugs Juliandra. "Anyway, tell me about your conversation with Carol."

"Ohh no, that's girl talk. Besides, you've heard it all before."

"Not really, plus I like hearing your voice, but you don't have to talk about it. I understand it was a part of your life that wasn't really that great and I tend to leave my early days in the dark to."

"Well, I'd like to think I've made peace with my past. It is what it is and nothing will change what happened. Without having gone through it, I wouldn't be who I am today."

"That's so true; sometimes I think about what I'd be like if I hadn't been exposed to so much turmoil in my youth."

"Yeah," Juliandra says, "it changes you, makes you see things differently and in some cases, opens your eyes to different paths."

"Indeed, it does! Before my parents divorced when I was ten, my brother and I were on a fast track to trouble. We were always causing mayhem. But, after they split, David was sent away to live with my dad and I became a lone soul. My whole world changed. I wasn't getting in trouble anymore because I was thinking for myself and seeing things my way for a change."

Juliandra puts her hand on Thomas's chest. "Oh baby, I'm surprised you don't do more with David now that you live in Maine."

"Yeah, me too, but everyone gets caught up in their own little world and time goes by so fast. It's not the same as when we were kids. We don't really have anything in common anymore. He grew up in Maine and kept getting into trouble, and I got stuck with my mother and I was constantly trying to avoid trouble. That woman exposed me to some terrible people and situations. I was dragged into bars where she would meet guys, brought to prisons to visit them when they got arrested for beating her or stealing, and I witnessed all the alcohol and drug activity I ever want to see. I'm so lucky I escaped that life without being physically abused in some way, it's not even funny. All those experiences though, have shaped and molded me. I have zero tolerance for drugs, alcohol or for anyone abusing another, and I try to be a decent role model for kids through the martial arts, so they can see that good people do exist. I'm not sure I'd be this way had I not been through all that."

"I think you would've turned out good no matter what, but probably you'd be doing different things. Maybe not really conscious of being a role model to kids or not going out of your way to be so protective of women."

"Maybe, I just feel what's right and what's wrong, and I don't like the wrong. Not in the least bit."

"I know Thomas, that's one of the reasons I love you so much. I could sense that when we first met. I knew that you would always protect me and always be there for me. Experiencing poverty most of my life makes me appreciate everything I have now, and experiencing all the not so great moments in my past really makes me enjoy the good times. It hurt losing my father at sixteen; it hurt me bad. I was kinda lost for a while and didn't know what direction to go. I just thought he would always be there. That changed me quite a bit and I made some poor choices back then. One of those poor choices was Craig, and I paid a high price for it. But, I've accepted that past and made my peace with it. The physical abuse from Craig and the trouble he caused by getting Brighten involved with drugs was horrible. Just like you though, those experiences molded me."

"And that's one of the reasons I love you so much. I could tell you were grounded and real, if you know what I mean. What I was seeing was the true you. There was no false image."

"Aww Thomas, I never knew that. You never told me that before."

"I never knew it before to be honest. It's taken years for me to understand why I love you the way I do, and talking about all this stuff made me think."

Juliandra kisses Thomas twice on the lips and pulls him out of bed and into the kitchen where she starts heating water for tea. She proposes they share some silly unknown facts about themselves, something each has yet to tell the other. This prompts Thomas to look at the microwave's clock. It's 9:16am, and with an odd look on his face he suggests taking the tea into the living room. The two grab their drinks, walk out of the kitchen and sit on the couch. Thomas starts to become distracted and preoccupied with thought. Anxiety begins to set in, and he keeps staring at a clock Juliandra put above the end table.

"What is up with you Thomas?" Juliandra asks. "Are you alright?"

His eyes move to her and back to the clock which he figures to now display 9:22. "Yeah, I'm fine."

"Do you want some breakfast? I'll go make you something."

"No, no I'm good right now; let's hang out in here. In fact, I feel like a little dancing."

"Ooh, now you're talking,"

Thomas reaches out with his left hand and as soon as Juliandra grabs it, he pulls her in for a slow dance. As he puts his right cheek to hers, the light smell of coconut from her hair alleviates his tension. "I love coconut," he says.

"I know," Juliandra replies. "That's why I use coconut conditioner."

The two move back and forth while Thomas starts to softly sing the lyrics to her favorite slow song. He's lost in her, and nothing else matters. *It's only the two of them,* he thinks, *alone together for a quiet weekend*. Thomas leans away, looks into her eyes, and places his right hand on her left cheek, then kisses her as if for the first time. The feelings hadn't changed and all he could think of is how much he wanted to be with her.

"Wow," Juliandra says, "that was nice! What brought that on?"

"I love you, that's all. I just love you more than you'll ever know."

"I love you too, Thomas. I love you very much. Now I am going to make some breakfast boy. What do you want?"

"How about some scrambled eggs? Ohh yeah, and you do know I lasted way more than thirty seconds."

Juliandra laughs as she walks towards the kitchen.

"Yeah, you're right; it was more like thirty five seconds."

Thomas smiles, shakes his head and catches a glimpse of that dreadful clock on the wall he hates so much. It takes a few seconds, but he deciphers the time to be about 9:35. Just as soon as his brain figures out the time, he calls out to Juliandra, who's almost to the kitchen. "Juliandra, come back for a second. Just real quick."

Juliandra stops and turns around. "What? Don't you want some eggs? Are you okay?"

At that moment, two windows in the living room shatter, raining glass onto the floor. Quickly, Thomas's eyes move from the clock on the wall to Juliandra's face then to the glass, and back to Juliandra. She's two steps in front of him, only two steps away when the look on her face changes. Her body, as if in slow motion, falls to the floor in the exact spot Thomas had pulled her to in his dream. And just as before, he rushes over and drops to his knees desperately trying to stop the blood from flowing out. Juliandra's life is fading quickly and with both arms, Thomas embraces her and yells out.

"No!"

He pulls back slightly to see her eyes as she tries to reach for him. Her arms simply drop to the floor. Her breath has stopped, her body is still, and her life is no more.

"Juliandra, no! Juliandra! I love you, Juliandra. Don't leave me!"

Thomas stares at her face for a moment crying, and yells again and again. "What is this? What is this?"

He frantically looks for his cell phone and finally sees it on the nightstand in the bedroom. After grabbing it and dialing 911, he tries to explain to the operator what he needs, but makes no sense while speaking. The operator decides to send emergency units to the location of the call and tells him to remain calm while help is on its way.

An ambulance shortly arrives along with a police car. Two EMTs rush to Juliandra's lifeless body.

Thomas is taken into custody by one officer and then brought to the local police station for questioning. Soon after arriving, he finds himself sitting in a plain room with a single table and two chairs. There's a camera on the wall and a blank notepad on the opposite side of the table. A man wearing dark clothing walks into the room. Thomas looks over and calls out his name.

"Detective Davis, I know you."

"You know me Mr. Lee? How do you know me?"

50

"You gave me your card. I had your card, with your name on it."

"I'm sorry, Mr. Lee, but if you had my card, I didn't give it to you. Where is this card?"

"I don't actually have it now, it was in my dream."

"Your dream? I gave you a card, in your dream?"

"Yes! This has happened before; at least I think it has. I had a nightmare and this happened!"

"Calm down, Mr. Lee. Tell me what happened in your home today?"

Thomas begins to describe everything to the detective and during his statement, explains the dream he had and how the events seemed to come true.

"You were the officer in my dream. You were there. What is this? How is this happening? Ohh my God, Juliandra."

Tears fall from Thomas's eyes.

"Mr. Lee, I have a team at your home right now working to find out what happened. We will learn the truth, but you need to tell me that truth. Alright, Thomas? Dreaming about something doesn't make it come true, do you understand me? People make things come true, not dreams. If you were involved in this I need to know now."

Just as Detective Davis finishes speaking, a skinny gentlemen, about six and a half feet tall walks into the room with a small bag, hands it to him and whispers in his ear. Detective Davis looks up at Thomas and tells him that they have found three bullet holes in the home, all from different weapons.

"I'm told, Mr. Lee, that three separate weapons seem to be involved in the death of your wife. We've found two entry points in the living room and one in the kitchen. We have also found a 7.62x51mm bullet lodged in the refrigerator. Do you know anyone with a rifle? Perhaps a US issued M40 rifle?"

"No, I don't know what the hell you're talking about. I don't have any guns and don't know anyone with a rifle."

"Mr. Lee, your wife was shot three times with high powered rifles. Are you telling me you know nothing about it, nothing at all?"

"All I know is that I was dancing with her in the kitchen, I mean living room. The kitchen was in my dream. Next thing I know, she's falling to the floor and dying in my arms. I couldn't stop the bleeding. I couldn't save her!"

"Here's how this is going to work, Thomas. You are a suspect as of right now. Although, considering what you've said today, I don't believe you had anything to do with it. What I believe, however, makes no difference. It's the evidence that will tell the story. You will be placed in protective custody until we sort this out. Two of my men will bring you to a hotel where you'll spend the night. You're not to leave that room for any reason. Do you understand?"

"Yes, yes I understand." Thomas replies. "Put me wherever, I don't really care anymore."

Detective Davis leaves Thomas in the room by himself. Moments later, two uniformed officers walk in and escort him to the rear of the building and out through a rusty metal door which leads to a parking lot. As the sun hits his face, all he can think of is the warmth of Juliandra that he'll never know again.

They make their way to an unmarked police cruiser where Thomas is placed in the back seat. Without small talk or pause, the car is started and driven away. Shortly after, they arrive at the Vacation Inn, located only two miles from the station. Both officers escort Thomas to room 316 on the third floor. One officer swipes the card key downward through the lock mechanism, opens the door, and enters to look around.

"It's all clear," he says, "let him in."

Thomas walks into the room with his head down and makes his way to the bathroom.

"We'll be right outside, Mr. Lee," explains one officer.

Thomas simply nods before closing the door. He looks in the mirror while reaching for the water faucet handle. A few splashes of cold water on his face and he looks again. Tears from his eyes flow down and become lost among the water droplets. *What is this... hell? Am I going crazy?*

"Regina!" he says out loud, "I've got to call her."

The bathroom door opens and Thomas rushes out. A small wooden desk where the room phone sits comes in to sight. He picks up the handset and dials her number. No answer. *She must be at the police station,* he thinks. He sprints to the room door, opens it, and tells the officers outside that he needs to see his mother-in-law, Regina Jones.

"I need to talk with her," he says. "She needs to know I had nothing to do with this. I need to speak with her as soon as possible."

One officer calls in and chats for a few minutes before explaining that the Detective, Regina and Brighten Jones are on their way to the hotel, and they will be there within two hours. As satisfied as anyone could possibly be in his situation, Thomas thanks the officers and goes back into the room where he reluctantly lies back on the single queen sized bed. *I've got to gather my thoughts,* he thinks. *I need to relax and think this through like a sane person.* Tears fall again from his eyes as he curls himself into a fetal position. After several minutes, he notices the sound of an analog clock sitting on the nightstand.

This was the kind of clock where the second hand jumped to the next position and bounced a little before it moved again. A loud tick could be heard with each second that went by. For some strange reason, the consistent and steady beat became soothing to his mind. Tick Tick Tick Tick. As the sound fades into the distance, nothingness begins to encompass the room until darkness takes over.

CHAPTER 5 - THE CHANGE

The sound of a small bird chirping interrupts the silence, like an alarm clock, and reminds Thomas that he's waiting for Regina to arrive at the Vacation Inn. Next, he feels the sensation of weight and warmth over his body, something he doesn't remember when lying down. His eyes open abruptly as he sits up and turns to his right.

"Juliandra!" he says out loud.

"What is it?" she replies.

Thomas immediately grabs his cell phone from the nightstand and looks at the time, 8:36am.

"What the hell?" he says. "This is crazy; this is absolutely insane!"

Within seconds he recalls, in vivid detail, the events that are on the way. If what he remembers is true, Juliandra will die one hour from now. *What do I do,* he thinks, *what do I do?* He embraces her and begins to kiss her several times on the cheek. "Juliandra, I love you so much, don't ever forget that."

"I love you too, Thomas. Now be quiet and cuddle with me for a while. Okay."

"Not now. We're getting the hell out of here."

"What are you talkin' about?"

Thomas springs out of the bed and looks at Juliandra with a very perplexed expression as if confused about what action to take.

"We have to leave Juliandra. We have to go right now."

"Thomas, stop playing around and get back in this bed."

"Juliandra, come with me, we've gotta get out of here. Grab your pants; come on, let's go!"

"Thomas, STOP IT! You're making me crazy. What's wrong with you?"

Out of the bedroom he runs, into the kitchen where he slips and falls onto the floor. While getting up the small display on the microwave comes into view. *Plenty of time,* he thinks. *It's only 8:40am.* He closes the blinds covering the kitchen windows and sprints out to the living room to do the same.

"Alright, now you can't see us. What's next?" he mumbles quietly.

Thomas looks down at the hand holding his cell phone. *911, of course, I'll call 911!* He dials, hesitates for a second, and hits the call button.

"911, what is your emergency?" A female voice asks.

"Someone's tryin' to kill my wife. They're going to shoot her!" He explains, frantic.

"Someone is trying to shoot your wife, sir? Can you tell me where this is happening? Do you have an address sir?"

"It's... Ahhh, it's 2408 Rosewater Avenue near downtown Bangor, 2408 Rosewater Avenue near downtown. Someone's going to shoot my wife if you guys don't get police here now. Please send the police."

"What's your name, sir? I need you to stay calm and please give me your name."

"Thomas, Thomas Lee and my wife is Juliandra Lee."

Juliandra, whose overheard Thomas talking on the phone, walks into the living room.

"Thomas, what's goin' on? Thomas, who are you talking to? Please Thomas; tell me you're joking around and this is just a prank."

"Sweetie, I'm on the phone with 911 and I'm trying to get the police out here."

911:
"Thomas, is everything alright? Mr. Lee, can you tell me what's going on?"

Thomas:
"Sorry, it's my wife, please send the police now."

Juliandra:
"What's going on Thomas? Talk to me, please."

Thomas:
"Juliandra, someone is going to try and kill you, and we need to go. I've lived through this already, we need to go now."

911:
"Mr. Lee, is someone there trying to hurt your wife right now?

Thomas:
"No... No, not yet. They're going to shoot her at 9:36."

911:
"Did someone call and threaten your wife, Mr. Lee? Can you tell me who's trying to hurt her?"

Thomas:

"I don't know who they are, all I know is they'll shoot her at 9:36."

911:

"Mr. Lee, I want you to remain calm. I have a two officers on the way to your location, okay? I need for you to stay calm."

Thomas:

"Yes... Yes, I am calm. I'm calm ma'am."

911:

"Officers should be there in less than ten minutes. Can you find a safe place to hide or go until they arrive?"

Thomas, thinking about the operator's question, looks at Juliandra who's in tears and still asking for answers. "The bathroom," he says out loud. "Juliandra, come on, we need to go into the bathroom and stay there."

"I'm not goin' anywhere until you tell me what's happening. What are you talking about?"

Thomas reaches out and grabs Juliandra by her arms near the shoulders.

"Listen, this is going to sound crazy, but someone, I don't know who, someone, is going to shoot you at 9:36, and we need to go to the bathroom and wait for the police to get here. Okay? Please... Trust me, when they arrive it'll all be fine."

He takes another look at the cell phone, which is still active and sees that it is now 8:49am.

"Okay, okay," Juliandra replies.

They head to the bathroom attached to the master bedroom which has only a small window that Thomas was supposed to change out for a larger one last summer. He leads Juliandra towards the freestanding cast iron tub.

"Let's get in; its iron and will stop bullets," he says.

Thomas steps over the side and pulls Juliandra in and downward to sit. Then, the sound of a distant voice calling his name changes his focus to the cell phone still connected to the emergency operator.

911:
"Mr. Lee, are you alright? Where are you now?"

Thomas:
In a whispering voice. "We're in the bathtub."

911:
"Officers should arrive in less than five minutes, Mr. Lee. Can I speak with your wife? I would like to check if she's alright."

Thomas:
"Yes, of course." Thomas hands the phone to Juliandra.

Juliandra:
"Hello?"

911:
"Juliandra Lee? Is that your name?"

Juliandra:
"Yes."

911:
"Juliandra, are you in danger?"

Juliandra:

"I don't know, my husband is acting crazy and says someone is trying to shoot me. We're in the bathroom, in the tub. I don't know what's going on and I'm scared."

911:

"Do you feel that your life is in danger from Thomas?"

Juliandra:

"No, he's just acting weird and thinks someone's going to kill me. He really believes it. I've never seen him this way, ever. He would never hurt me."

Suddenly, they hear a loud thumping at the front door. It was the sound made when knocking with the side of your fist rather than the knuckles.

Thump Thump Thump

A muffled but loud voice calls out. "Thomas Lee, its Bangor P.D."

Thump Thump Thump

"Mr. Lee, I need you to answer the door. It's Bangor P.D. We were dispatched by 911 to this address."

"Finally!" Thomas says as he turns to Juliandra. "Alright, stay here, okay?"

Thomas makes his way to the front door where he looks through the glass pane and sees, much to his relief, two uniformed officers standing outside. He opens the door and finds one of the officers has removed his firearm from the holster and is holding it, pointed downward. The other, moves slightly to his left as the door opens and stands with his right hand above his weapon.

"Mr. Lee? We've been dispatched here because you called 911. May we come in?"

"Yes please," Thomas says, "come in."

"I'm going to need you to step outside for me, Mr. Lee. Please place your hands on top of your head and step through the front door towards my partner here."

Thomas complies and walks out in the direction of the second officer.

"I'm going to enter your home now, Mr. Lee, and make sure your wife is alright. Please stay outside with Officer Mitchell."

The first Officer takes a step into the entryway and calls for Juliandra, making sure his firearm is not out, but can be quickly accessed.

"Mrs. Lee? Juliandra, ma'am, can you please come to the front door?"

Juliandra hears the officer call out and quickly heads towards him.

"Mrs. Lee, I'm Officer Daniels with Bangor P.D. and we've been dispatched here because your husband called 911. Are you alright?"

"Yes, yes I am, but I don't know what's happening. My husband keeps telling me that someone's going to shoot me."

"Ma'am, is anyone here now that is trying to hurt you?"

"No, it's just me and Thomas."

"Mrs. Lee, I would like to come in and check around; is that alright with you?"

"Yes, please."

"Okay, I need for you to step outside with your husband and Officer Mitchell, alright? I'm going to take a look around."

Officer Daniels enters the living room and begins to check through the rest of the house. After walking through each room he verbally checks in with Officer Mitchell, who's still standing on the porch with Thomas and Juliandra. What feels like an eternity goes by before Officer Daniels approaches the front door again and waves to Officer Mitchell, signaling him to bring everyone inside.

Officer Mitchell holsters his firearm but keeps his hand above it as he asks both Juliandra and Thomas to step into the house towards Officer Daniels.

"Please have a seat guys," says Officer Mitchell.

Officer Daniels speaks up. "Okay, I have checked your home and found no one else here. Can you explain to me why we're here, Mr. Lee?"

Before answering, Thomas looks in the direction of the oversized wall clock and pauses to take note of the time; 9:00am, which for once is easily read because the hands are pointed right at the numbers.

"Officer, I know this is going to sound ridiculous and crazy, but someone is going to shoot my wife at 9:36."

"Who is going to shoot your wife, and how do you know what time it will happen?"

"I don't know who, I just know that it's going to happen, at 9:36, someone is going to shoot my wife."

"Did someone threaten her, Mr. Lee?"

"No, I don't know. I just know they're gonna do it."

"Mr. Lee, I need for you to look at me. Have you had any alcohol last night or this morning?"

"No… No, I don't drink at all, nothing at all."

"Have you taken any unknown substances or drugs that you're aware of? Any medications or prescriptions?"

"No, I don't take anything. I don't use drugs or medications."

"Okay, Mr. Lee, I'd like you to accompany me outside while Mrs. Lee remains in the house with Officer Mitchell and answers a few questions."

The two walk outside and Officer Daniels starts to explain that it's a serious offence to make prank calls to 911 and that it is important not to have them wasting time while real crimes are occurring.

Meanwhile, Officer Mitchell is asking Juliandra to explain the morning's events in detail for him. Juliandra tells the officer that Thomas has never acted this way and she has never known him to take drugs or drink alcohol. A few minutes go by then Thomas and Officer Daniels walk back into the home.

"Alright Mrs. Lee, can you please change your clothes and accompany us to the station? Your husband is hell bent on going with us and we need to get back to work."

Juliandra stands up and makes her way to the bedroom. She swaps her pajamas for a pair of black slacks and a white button shirt while Thomas quickly changes and heads to the front door to wait. After looking again at the clock over the couch, he sees the time, 9:25am, then becomes very nervous and starts to rush things. Both of them follow the officers outside where they get into Thomas's older truck which has slowly changed in color from black to red-orange due to rust. Thomas puts the key in the ignition switch and tries to start the engine. It turns over but won't run. He tries three more times before giving up and hitting the steering wheel.

"You need a new truck," Juliandra says. "I'll grab my keys and we can take my car."

"Quick, Juliandra, quick!" Thomas says, frantically. "We need to move fast!"

Thomas keeps looking at the time on his phone and watches as the digits change to 9:30. He gets out of the truck and Officer Mitchell walks over.

"Truck won't start?" He asks.

Thomas replies, "No, it won't. We're going to get her keys and take the car instead."

Juliandra is already on her way back out of the house with her keys and walks to the driver's side of her pearl colored Honda. The two quickly get in and Juliandra inserts the key then rotates it forward, but just as Thomas's truck, the engine turns without starting. She tries a couple more times before Thomas exits the vehicle and steps around to the front of it. He asks Juliandra to pull the hood release lever. Office Daniels walks over to the car just as Thomas lifts the hood and begins to look around.

"Looks like someone's cut your plug wires. I think both of you should get in our vehicle. Right now."

Just as Juliandra looks at the car radio's screen which displays 9:35am, Thomas rushes over to the driver side door, opens it and pulls her out.

"Come on, let's go!" he says. "We need to get in the cruiser."

Officer Mitchell opens the rear door on the driver's side to let Juliandra in while Thomas rushes to the passenger side and sits beside her. They look at each other with relief as if they've just finished a marathon then Thomas notices the time on the cruiser's computer screen, 9:35. He realizes the time set in Juliandra's car radio is a couple of minutes off and begins to look around outside the windows. Officers Daniels and Mitchell are just getting into the front seats as the time on the cruiser's computer screen changes to 9:36.

Glass from the windshield suddenly hits Thomas's face as Officer Daniel's grabs his neck. The rear window shatters dispersing small fragments everywhere, and Juliandra cries out with a short burst of air then falls forward. At the moment Thomas yells, "Ohh my God!" The side window explodes into hundreds of pieces that coat the entire back seat. He looks down at his arm, which has started to bleed, and then turns towards Juliandra. She's not moving at all and the white shirt she put on moments ago has almost entirely turned red. Thomas, now partially covered in blood is holding her tight with his right hand on her neck and left hand on her heart.

Officer Daniels, unable to speak, is lying back in his seat with both hands tight to his neck. Officer Mitchell is calling for backup, remaining low in his seat and making sure to hide his head from view of the windshield.

"Officer down, officer down, we are under fire!" He repeats "2408 Rosewater Ave, approach with caution, snipers in the area. 2408 Rosewater Ave. Approach with caution, there are snipers in the area! Officer Daniels is severely wounded. We need to get him out of here."

He looks back to assess the condition of Thomas and Juliandra then continues. "One civilian is dead and the other..."

Sounds become muffled as Thomas holds Juliandra and stares straight ahead in disbelief.

"Why is this happening to me?" he says aloud. "Why?"

Suddenly, his expression changes while his gaze pierces through a broken window. The look of disbelief and confusion turns to one of determination. Every emotion swirling around in his head starts to converge and form only one feeling: Anger.

Life has no meaning anymore, he thinks. *My life has no meaning without her. I'm in hell.*

Officer Mitchell reaches back to Thomas. "Are you okay? Are you shot?"

Thomas doesn't answer, but continues to stare out into the distance, holding tight to Juliandra's body. The world begins to fade as memories of the first day they met flood back.

It was six years ago...

CHAPTER 6 - THE FIRST TIME

Music was blaring while Thomas watched two friends bounce back and forth to the ear piercing beat produced by a band he wasn't that crazy about. The group was one of four sharing the stage at a concert that night in the Springfield Massachusetts Civic Center. Thomas was only interested in the fourth band playing later on. A push here and a shove there kept him on constant guard while trying to pretend his ears didn't hurt from the speakers only twenty feet away.

His friend Richard insisted on being right in front of the stage, so the three arrived early and battled the crowd for position. You had to try and hold your ground, but the people were like an ocean carrying waves of powerful force which made you move whether you wanted to or not. Every now and then a funnel opened up, and you would do everything possible to avoid being drawn into a sinkhole called a mosh pit where people collide with one another just for fun.

Luckily, the third band's set was almost over and Thomas's reason for being there in the first place would be taking the stage. Before finishing their last song, the lead singer decided to let a young boy from the crowd join him on stage. He let the kid hold a guitar while his dad took a picture. *The young kid shouldn't have been at a concert like that*, Thomas thought, *but how nice the guy let him on stage.* After a bit of goofing around, the young boy was led off, and the lead singer announced that the next song would be their last. He also called out for the crowd to split down the middle and create two groups which would run towards each other when told. Something the band called "The wall of death."

Thomas had thought, *Ohh, just great... Can't wait for this group of drunk, high, and uncoordinated individuals to run towards and bash into another group of drunk, high, and uncoordinated individuals. What could possibly go wrong there?*

He started moving to the left side of the pit, saw a large gap opening in the center and couldn't help but feel like a cow being herded somewhere.

This is the last hard rock concert I'll attend, Thomas thought. *If I survive, that's it; I'm stayin' home from now on. I made it all the way to this point and now we're going to run into each other like morons and get smashed.*

Thomas lost his view of Richard, but was pretty sure he was at the very front, ready to collide and rumble with the other side. The band started jamming and the lead singer was yelling out lyrics like he was angry at the microphone. Suddenly, the music stopped, and he yelled: "GO!"

"Crap," Thomas said out loud. "Already?"

The mass of people he was stuck with gave him no choice but to run towards the other mass of people only feet away. There was no stopping that momentum. He knew if he tried to stay still, he would have been trampled. It'd be better to flow with the force and try not to fight it. To his surprise and delight, no one was hurt and he may have actually enjoyed the adrenaline rush. The band left the stage while Thomas was swimming through the ocean of bodies back towards the front. He wanted to see the final group up close knowing it will be worth the effort. Much of the crowd had been drinking and smoking throughout the concert, so the level of rowdiness continued to escalate. Thomas just kept telling himself that it would be worth it.

Twenty-two minutes of "excuse me, excuse me, I'm sorry, pardon me" and trying to catch a breath of air not filled with the smell of marijuana was beginning to take its toll, but finally the last band took the stage. The first song started without warning, and the crowd turned back as the lead singer rose from a moving platform behind everyone. *Now that's cool*, Thomas thought as he smiled and moved around to the beat.

Three songs in and the people had started crowd surfing from the back to the front of the pit. Some were lucky enough to make it all the way, but some were not and were left to kiss the ground as they get tossed in the air with no one to catch them. *That's gotta hurt,* Thomas kept thinking. *Man that has got to hurt when you're seven feet high and just plop to the ground on your back or neck, ouch!* He couldn't help but be mesmerized by the people risking life and limb for a totally unsafe joy ride to the stage. He realized that the odds of making it all the way were about one in three. Enjoying the sideshow with some great tunes had made the situation tolerable. Thomas looked to the left and then to the right for more people riding the waves of hands. A quick look behind and **BAM!** Thomas immediately grabbed his nose.

"My nose! My nose!" He said. "Damn! Damn it!"

Blood poured out as he held it and uncontrollable tears had begun to flow from his eyes. As bad as it hurt though, he thought more about how embarrassing it was to look like he was crying.

"Ahhh, this sucks," he mumbled as a little space formed around the unfortunate projectile that landed on his face and broke his nose. Thomas tried to focus with the endless supply of tears spilling from his eyes, and finally, after blinking twenty times in a row, was able to see. The projectile was a thin girl wearing a light pink hoodie, blue jeans, and black boots with extra thick soles, lying on her back laughing. The girl was helped up by a couple of drunken crowd members while she looked around to get her bearings. She saw Thomas covering his face while blood dripped down his hands and arms.

"Ohh my God!" She said. "Did my shoe do that?"

Thomas looks down at her boots, back up to her face, and simply nodded his head.

"I think my nose is broken," he yelled out over the music.

The girl, still with a hood over her head, grabbed his arm and pulled him out of the crowd to the left towards a corral space reserved as the concert's triage center. Another poor guy holding his nose was walking back into the mob of bouncing fans as they were leaving, so Thomas gave him a thumbs-up as they passed each other. A few people with staff t-shirts seemed to be prepared for injuries and had plenty of large gauze type bandages to hand out. One staff member gave the girl two and a cold bottle of water to help clean up the blood. They took a seat in the corral where the girl dropped her hood back, ripped open one of the bandages, and poured cold water on it. She proceeded to pluck Thomas's hands away to see the extent of damage her shoe caused.

"Ouch, that looks like it hurts... I'm so sorry," she said. "Try to stay still. I have a little medical training and I'm gonna clean up your nose, okay?"

Thomas was in awe as he noticed every detail of the girls face and skin. Again he nodded while the girl wiped away the blood from his upper lip. Her black hair was long, but she had it pulled back in three cornrows on the left side just above her ear. Thomas thought it looked really nice. It showed off her perfect ear, perfect nose, and perfect lips.

"What's your name?" She asked.

"Thomas," he replied.

"Well Thomas, I'm Juliandra and my friends dared me to try crowd surfing tonight, and I really thought that I was gonna make it all the way up to the stage. I guess I was wrong, huh?"

"Yeah, but you probably didn't expect a giant nose to block your ride," Thomas said as he tried to smile.

Juliandra giggled and continued to wipe his face. "Ahh... Well, your nose isn't that big. I think my foot may have pushed it in a couple of inches so you're not half bad looking now."

Thomas chuckled and thanked her for the help as she unwrapped the second bandage and separated it into two pieces.

"It's the least I can do, Thomas. After all, my foot has already made out with your face, so we're practically dating, right?"

Thomas laughed causing his nose to start gushing blood again. Juliandra took the two pieces of gauze and held them out.

"I want you to keep your head back and put one piece of gauze in each nostril to stop the bleeding." She said. "I'd do it, but I only go so far on a first date, and plugging nostrils is where I draw the line."

Thomas took the gauze and proceeded to shove both pieces in his nose then turned to look at her and smiled.

"At least we can still enjoy the music from here," he said. "I bet you didn't think you'd be on a first date with someone that looked like this."

"You're right; I was hoping I would've landed on a big, ruggedly handsome man with gauze stickin' out of a smaller nose."

Both smiled and continued to talk for the rest of the concert as if the music was nothing more than a radio playing in the background. It took a while, but Thomas was finally able to remove the gauze and wipe his face clean which allowed him to continue the conversation with some dignity. He learned that Juliandra had driven to the Springfield Civic Center from Maine just as he did with his friends. She was studying to become a nurse, and currently doing clinicals at Eastern Maine Medical Center, but was thinking about working to help people break their addiction to drugs.

"I've seen the damage it does firsthand," she explained, "and I've seen the hopes and dreams of my brother, Brighten, lost and forgotten. I just want to help people. Even if I can only help one person, you know?"

"I understand," Thomas replied. "I came from a not so great family life where I was around people who drank morning, noon, and night, did drugs, and committed theft. Somehow, I came outta that okay and I try to teach kids good values through martial arts because it helped me a lot. I don't like to drink and I'll never use drugs. I just don't believe they're good for anyone."

"You're a good man, Thomas."

"I try," he said.

"Now, I just have one question…"

"What's that?"

"Well, if you teach martial arts, shouldn't you have seen my shoe coming? You know, ninja stuff, like poof! And you're out of the way, then Hi-Yah!"

Thomas just laughed. "Well, I'm gonna have to work on my skills, no doubt about that."

As the crowd thinned, the two parted ways to meet up with their friends, but agreed to regroup after the concert to talk more. A while later, Thomas walked into a local all-night diner to see that Juliandra and her three girlfriends had arrived first, and were sitting in a large corner booth waiving to him and his friends. He walked towards the booth and told the girls that he needed to get washed up in the bathroom and would be right back. After washing his face and hands, Thomas looked in the mirror and thought he was almost good as new, outside of the swollen nose and bloodstains riddling his shirt. He made his way out and over to the booth where the girls were laughing at something Richard said.

The questions really started to fly once they got past some awkward small talk, and after a few more laughs from Richard's dorky comments, it turned out to be the best night of Thomas's life. His broken nose was a small price to pay for the chance to meet such a wonderful girl. The more he learned about her, the more he wanted to know, and the more he just couldn't keep his eyes away. *How could someone so beautiful be so nice and awesome?* He kept thinking.

Every girl he had ever dated up until that moment was a nightmare. He always expected one thing but got another, and was either friend zoned or used in some way by all of them. He remembered his thoughts drifting a bit that night as he reviewed some of the unsuccessful dating attempts from the past. One in particular named Audrey came to mind. She had asked to borrow his car, and he let her thinking it would score some points. Maybe it would lead to a date or something he thought. Unfortunately, when she returned the vehicle and thanked him, she started talking about how important it was to get a phone to her boyfriend before lunch.

That was the last time that ever happened. He went further back in time to remember another girl named Sean, an old co-worker, who would give him rides home because he didn't have a car back then. She flirted with him throughout the day and they bantered back and forth constantly. One night when she drove him home, he asked if she wanted to kiss. She simply smiled and said that her boyfriend probably wouldn't like that.

Wow! He thought. *If you've got a boyfriend, why are you flirting with me every day?*

He was too embarrassed to say anything as he opened the car door, got out, and walked away. It was the last ride home he ever accepted from a girl. His mind continued to go even further back. Second grade and Thomas was playing outside. It was free time during school and all the kids were running around, jumping rope, and playing kickball. He was kicking rocks around by a tree when a girl he had a crush on named Robin came right up to him.

"I heard from Joey that you liked me, Thomas." She said.

"Yeah, I do." He replied.

Robin put her arms down by her sides, took a breath, and loudly belted out "Well, I don't like you!" Ouch!

His mindset shifted again to analyzing all those social failures and then suddenly his inner voice screamed out *"Oh My God! Do I have some kind of complex from the past? Holy crap, I have to let this stuff go and move on!"* Those bad experiences which made him all but give up on finding the perfect girl, that special one, that person you think you're supposed to be with, your soul mate, are now in the past. The sound of Juliandra's voice drew him away from his stray thoughts and made him forget about every other girl he'd ever met. The group's conversation continued on for over two hours before everyone had paid and begun to make their way outside.

God, I hope this girl doesn't have a boyfriend, he thought while walking out the door. Once in the parking lot he and Juliandra were pulled away by their friends, but each resisted to get a few last words in. Juliandra's group was staying at a nearby hotel but Thomas and his friends had driven to the concert with the intention of going home that night.

A moment of awkwardness occurred and Thomas tried to get the nerve to ask Juliandra if he could call when she got back to Maine.

"Come on, Thomas, let's go." Richard barked out. "We've got a long ass ride ahead of us."

"Hold on, hold on. I just wanna ask Juliandra a quick question."

"Ohh, really? A quick question, Loverboy? Are you in love, Thomas? Ohh, that is so… Cute!"

"Umm, you guys can head to the car and I'll catch up."

Richard crossed his arms and stood firm.

"Uhh, no can do, bro. I have to hear this, so I can judge and make fun of you later. Make no mistake; I will judge you, and I will make fun of you. You may ask your question, sir."

Thomas pushed him off balance. "Alright, asshole!"

He looked at Juliandra and took a deep breath.

"Juliandra, I was wondering if we could maybe umm..."

Richard interrupted, laughing, "Get it on! Ride the wave maybe?"

"Ahhh, you butthole! Shut up! GOD! You're such a dink!"

Juliandra, also started to laugh then handed Thomas a card.

"My number's on the back. I'd love to talk again. I'll be back in Bangor on Monday, but won't have any time until Wednesday. Just give me a call, okay."

Thomas smiled and Richard started bumping him along continuing his laughter.

"You're going to be a man someday, Thomas, I can feel it."

He put the card in his pocket and looked at Richard.

"Well, you're an asshole right now, Richard, and we can all feel it! Oooohhh, does it hurt? Ahhhwww."

CHAPTER 7 - THE QUESTIONS

Reality smacks Thomas right in the face as the doors to the police car suddenly open and he's pulled out and separated from Juliandra. EMTs are on the scene and one looking him over calls out.

"Let's get him in the ambulance. It's only a minor wound!"

Two others begin examining Juliandra and another two are already checking out Officer Daniels. Uniformed officers have filled the street as quickly as the blood filled the white canvas of Juliandra's shirt, and Thomas couldn't help but think the entire police force was right there on that one road. He sits, eyes darting back and forth, watching armed men and women move door to door searching homes. A detail comes to mind, 7.62x51, the caliber of bullet Detective Davis mentioned during his interrogation. How terrible he thought, to know the exact specifications of what killed his wife, but to not know how to save her from it?

He can see Officer Daniels taken away in an ambulance moments before Juliandra's body gets moved into another one. Seconds later, the view keeping him informed is abruptly blocked when a young policeman steps into the back of his ambulance and the rear doors are closed. The vehicle starts moving and soon Thomas finds himself under the care of Nurse Rachel whom he remembers clearly from before.

It was extremely tempting to acknowledge her familiarity, but not this time. Silence is the new theme. Offer only what's necessary to try and figure out how to beat this thing; this hell controlling his life. It isn't going to win. He's going to observe and find its weakness, a way out, a clue; anything.

The nurse finishes wrapping his arm with fresh gauze.

"How's that, Mr. Lee? Is it too tight?"

"No, it's fine. It's really good, thank you."

"You're welcome," she replies.

"Is there any way you can get the officer that brought me in? I really need to talk with him."

"Oh, I think I can find him for you. I don't believe he's very far away."

A smile forms on her face as she walks towards the door. "I'll get Officer Richards for you. Try not to move your arm around too much. Even though its only five stitches, excessive movement could cause the wound to open up again. I'll be back in a few minutes to check on you, okay?"

A small nod from Thomas and the nurse is gone, but before he has a chance to drift away in thought, young Officer Richards enters the room and approaches.

"Officer Richards," Thomas says. "Officer, I need to speak with Detective Ron Davis as soon as possible. Can we go to the station? I need to talk to him now."

"Sir, as soon as the doctor discharges you, we can head down to the station. You can make a full statement, and a Detective will be assigned to you. Do you know Detective Davis?"

"No, I just know of him and would like to consult with him," Thomas replies. It was going to be difficult to stick to his new theme, but how crazy would it have sounded to explain?

"I'm not sure Detective Davis will be assigned to your case, but I'll let him know you want to speak with him. I'm going to check with the doctor and see about your discharge and we'll go from there."

Officer Richards walks out of the room and Thomas starts looking it over, identifying objects. An older rolling stool that could use a new layer of vinyl is off to the left, and the stainless steel sink built in to the counter seems very clean. A partially open drawer is filled with gauze, wrapped tubes, what looks like Popsicle sticks, and a single roll of white tape.

Before he could move on to the next object Officer Richards is once again standing in front of him, almost as if he had never left.

"Mr. Lee, the doctor's informed me that you're being discharged. You'll need to sign a couple of things on the way out. Just follow me and we can get you out of here."

Thomas pushes off the examination bed and onto his feet right behind the officer now leading him out the door. They arrive at a desk where Nurse Rachel is chatting with another nurse beside a computer screen. She pauses and immediately smiles, making eye contact with Thomas, then reminds him not to bend his arm too much as she hands over a few papers.

"Normally, you would see much more of me, Mr. Lee, but these are unusual circumstances, and we're releasing you into the charge of Officer Richards. Please initial here and here then sign right here."

Thomas remains silent, simply nodding to acknowledge her instructions. He signs the papers and hands them back before falling in line behind Officer Richards who is now navigating his way out of the building to a squad car. Two men are already in the front seats and Officer Richards escorts Thomas to rear passenger door, opens it, and steps aside so he can get in.

"These officers are going to take you to the station, Mr. Lee, where you can give a statement and speak to the investigator who has been assigned to your case. His name is Detective Ronald Davis."

In a quick motion Thomas looks up at the officer with slightly widened eyes and nods as the door closes. The hospital begins to shrink into the landscape as the car accelerates forward and only minutes later the police station comes in to view, getting larger and larger until the car stops.

Thomas is escorted to an office where Detective Davis is waiting. *This is different than before,* he thinks. *Last time, I was a criminal suspect and treated like dirt. Now, I'm a guest.*

"Have a seat, Mr. Lee. I'm Detective Davis and I've been assigned to your case. I know this is a difficult time for you, but it's extremely important that we get as much information as we can as soon as possible before memories become skewed. I hope you understand."

"I understand, Detective." Thomas replies.

"Okay, I need to record your statements, Mr. Lee. Do you also understand that what you say will be recorded for later review?"

"Yes."

Detective Davis walks over to a video camera mounted on a tripod and lines up Thomas in its view.

"Alright, I'm going to start the camera recording and then I'll ask you a few questions."

A small red light comes on and Detective Davis walks back to his chair, sits down then begins a series of questions written on his notepad.

"Can you please state your name and age?" He asks.

"My name is Thomas Benjamin Lee, and I'm 32 years old."

"What is your place of residence?"

"I live at 2408 Rosewater Avenue, in Bangor, Maine."

A few more general questions follow before the Detective finally asks Thomas to explain, in detail, the events of that morning. Thomas looks down for a moment and then raises his eyes to meet the Detective's. A deep breath and he begins describing everything, in as much detail as possible, without mentioning anything that could make him sound crazy. The detective is patient and lets Thomas recount all events without interruption, until he comes to the present moment.

"Mr. Lee, I'm looking at a transcript from your 911 call today. The 911 operator asked you if someone threatened your wife and you said: 'I don't know who they are, all I know is they will shoot her at 9:36.' Can you help me understand this statement and how exactly you knew someone was going to shoot your wife? How did you know this was going to happen precisely at 9:36?"

Realizing that this one small detail could change the way he's treated and would lead to him being held at the station, Thomas thinks about what to say for a moment. He remembers dropping his cell phone during the chaos and takes a gamble it hadn't been recovered yet. He tells the Detective that he received an anonymous text message stating Juliandra would be shot at 9:36am.

"I took it seriously," he explains. "Juliandra works with lots of drug addicts and I just assumed it was a drug dealer or gang member. I don't know who sent it. I just believed it."

"Where's your cellphone now, Mr. Lee?"

"I don't know. I left it at the house or dropped it at some point this morning when we were trying to leave."

"I believe it'll be found soon, in fact, the phone is probably somewhere in the station now. Our guys are thorough, and as soon as I can get it we can confirm this message. I want you to know that I'm very sorry for your loss, Mr. Lee. This is a tragedy, and I'll do my best to find out who is responsible, but for me to do so, I need facts... Clear facts."

An older gentleman dressed in a grey suite knocks on the office door and enters with a manila folder in his right hand. Detective Davis gets up and turns off the camera before walking over and taking it. He sits down again, opens the folder, and begins to read.

"What is it?" Thomas asks. "Do you have any information on the killers?"

"No, I'm afraid not, this is a report from Officer Mitchell, and some notes from the examiner. I asked them to rush me their findings as soon as they could. According to the examiner's notes, your wife was hit with three separate bullets."

Without thinking, Thomas blurts out, "7.62?"

"Yes, how did you know that?" the detective asks.

"Well, that's a common caliber for sniper rifles, isn't it?"

"Yes, it is a common round and two of the three that were recovered are 7.62x51mm. The third hasn't been identified. It was larger, possibly an 8.6x70mm, also known as a .338 Lapua Magnum. Those have a long range and can be effective at 2,000 plus yards, depending on conditions. The 7.62, however, has a much shorter range, somewhere around 400 yards max. This makes our job very hard, Mr. Lee, very hard indeed. But, I've got good men out there searching for evidence that may lead us to the shooters."

"Jesus… 400 yards? 2,000 yards? They could've been anywhere. They could be long gone by now. How the hell are you guys gonna find them?"

"We have two of the bullets. We'll have the trajectory of each soon, which will tell us approximately where those two gunmen were when they pulled the trigger. We'll have your threatening text message that can be traced. We have a small town where not much goes unnoticed, and we have some of the best people in law enforcement working on this. We'll find them. Trust me. Now, you need a place to stay. Do you have somewhere you can go tonight?"

"My mother-in-law, Regina," Thomas replies. "I should stay with her."

"I believe she's here now, with her son. I'll need to speak with them as well before you leave."

Detective Davis picks up a phone on the desk, hits a button, and asks to have an officer sent to him.

"Thomas," he says, "I'm going to have you go with one of our men until I finish speaking with Mrs. Jones. I'll let you know when I'm done."

In walks the now familiar face of Officer Richards, who seems to get younger every time Thomas sees him.

"Ahh... Officer Richards, can you please take Mr. Lee to get some coffee?"

With a serious look and perfect posture, the youthful officer replies, "Yes sir," then waits for Thomas to stand. Both walk out, make their way past a reception area, and end up at the entrance of a room containing a vending machine, small coffee maker, a few tables, and several chairs that have seen better days. Before entering, Thomas turns and sees Detective Davis walking towards Regina who's sitting in the lobby, sobbing, while Brighten holds her in his arms. Brighten is looking upward and blinking often, trying to prevent tears from falling as he holds his lips tight to stop them from quivering. Thomas recalls Juliandra saying he was a proud man. He could see that now, in the way Brighten held himself. Too proud he thought. Too proud to bend an inch for the sadness of losing his sister, not even this horrible tragedy could break that pride.

Officer Richards shows Thomas the coffee and instructs him to remain in that room until Detective Davis comes for him.

"I really don't drink coffee, Officer; can I just get a cup of water?"

The officer points to a water cooler in the far corner.

"There's a vending machine in here as well if you get hungry, sir."

84

Knowing he has no money for the vending machine, Thomas simply thanks the officer and walks over to get a drink. He fills a cup, sits down and starts to think about what Detective Davis said earlier regarding facts. Facts are the key, and he needs to get all the facts.

Who, what, when, where, and why? He thinks. *Who we don't know yet, could be gang members, but no... This was too organized. Drug dealers could have done this; she works against them every day. Of course they would kill her. Maybe Brighten is involved. He used to be into drugs and knows people. Maybe a hit on his sister to teach him a lesson? Damn it! Who?*

Almost 45 minutes go by before Regina, Brighten, and Detective Davis walk in. Thomas stands up and puts his cup down before taking a small step forward. Regina, still crying, and wiping tears from underneath her eyes, reaches out and walks directly toward him.

"Regina," Thomas says as he wraps his arms around her, "I couldn't save her. I tried, but I couldn't save her."

"I know Thomas, I know."

Brighten remains at the doorway, back stiff, his arms crossed, and a facial expression molded by hate, anger, and suspicion. Detective Davis speaks:

"Thomas, Mrs. Jones has agreed to let you stay with her. We'll have an unmarked car follow you out, and they'll be watching her place overnight. I need for everyone to stay home and NOT leave the area. If anyone needs something critical, let the officers know, and we'll have someone get it for you. Now, hang tight here for a few moments and I'll send over the officers who'll be looking out for you."

Detective Davis leaves the room and Brighten springs forward taking the opportunity to grill Thomas for answers.

"What's going on, Thomas? What are you into that got my sister killed, huh? What kind of shit are you involved with?"

"Nothing, Brighten, I tried to save her. I did everything I could to save her life. The question should be, what are you into that got her killed? Some drug deal gone wrong? Maybe you pissed off the wrong people, and Juliandra paid for it! Maybe some of your home boys did this!"

"You cracker mother fucker! I know this is your fault and you're gonna pay! Juliandra should have never been with you! She deserved better than you! You're just some white fuckin' asshole who thinks you're better than us, and you've got no place in our family! **No place!**"

"Let me get this straight you cocaine sucking idiot. You dragged Juliandra into your shit world of drugs, alcohol, and crime, where she had to save your stupid ass, and pull you, Brighten, a sorry waste of fucking space and useless human being, back from the pits of that hell hole of a life, if that's what anyone would call it. She was torn to pieces watching you destroy yourself and your family, and I have done nothing but make her happy. You come at me with that? You fuckin' piece of shit! If anyone's to blame, it's you and your crack shooting fucking friends!"

"Juliandra is my sister, and my kind, boy! Not your kind! Not for you. Never for you! We were fine before you, and you don't belong!"

It was at that point Thomas realized race was only an excuse for his anger. In Brighten's mind he had taken his sister away, and

Brighten needed her; he needed her to keep him on the right path. Now, she's gone forever, and he was scared.

"You know what, Brighten?" Thomas says. "What about Juliandra? What about what Juliandra wanted? I do belong because she chose me. That's what she wanted. She loved me, and she loved you, so it doesn't matter what you think. No one stopped you from being part of her life. That was all you. Don't blame me for your mistakes, because she was happy."

"ENOUGH!" Regina shouts. "That is... enough! Juliandra is gone; my baby's gone and I will not have you two going at it. Juliandra was a grown ass woman and she did what she wanted. She was where she wanted to be. End of story! Get that? Enough of this!"

Silence falls over the room as Regina steps towards the water cooler and takes a seat at a small white table. Brighten walks over to the coffee machine and again crosses his arms. Five minutes go by and not one word is uttered from any of them. Finally, the silence is broken when Detective Davis walks in with two men wearing suits in tow, one middle aged, and the other closer to retirement by the looks.

"Mrs. Jones, Mr. Lee, Mr. Jones, this is Officer Williams and Officer Walker. They will be escorting you home and watching your place tonight. I will contact you when we get more details on what has happened."

Detective Davis hands each of them a card and asks that they call if any new information comes to mind. The two suited officers escort Thomas, Brighten, and Regina out of the building and to her car. Thomas climbs in the back as Brighten opens the front passenger door and mumbles under his breath.

"Yeah, you better get in the back, boy."

As soon as Brighten sits, Thomas leans forward.

"At least I have a license to drive Brighten; I can sit in the driver's seat of a car. How about you?"

Brighten quickly turns, ready to fire back, but is interrupted by Regina.

"If I hear one more word from either of you two children, I'll beat your asses with my shoe until you can taste my feet! Now, shut the hell up!"

Regina starts the car and follows the unmarked police cruiser all the way home. Once there, she invites the two officers inside for coffee while Brighten and Thomas make their way inside to the kitchen table.

"I'm sorry," Thomas says to Brighten. "I didn't mean all those things I said back at the police station; I'm angry and just want to know what happened."

"Oh, you meant every word, Thomas, but despite what you think, I was only a user of drugs, I never dealt them."

"Well, can you think of anyone who'd do this? Anyone? Was anybody mad at you or upset enough to do this?"

"Still on me, eh? You just can't accept the fact that a black man wasn't dealing drugs huh? Why is that, Thomas?"

"No, that's not it at all Brighten. I know Juliandra worked with some pretty shady characters at the center; characters capable of anything. I just thought that since you were once..."

"Once what? A druggy? An addict? You thought I'd know everything about those who deal drugs, commit crimes and murder people?"

"Jesus, man; I'm just trying to figure out what's goin' on. Can you stop being defensive for a second?"

Meanwhile, the officers have left the house and gone outside to their car, and Regina is finishing off a bottle of wine in the living room while looking through an old photo album. She calls Brighten and Thomas to see some of the pictures. Both make their way to the couch, sit, and listen to her tell stories of Juliandra's past as she flips through several pages.

The more Regina refills her glass, the more random her stories become, and the less sense they make. Thomas and Brighten are actively trying not to pay attention, but her voice is becoming louder and harder to ignore though.

"Boys, did you know that Juliandra was born ugly?" She says.

Brighten and Thomas, suddenly look at Regina.

"It's true, Ohh Lord, she was an ugly child. I knew when she was born that she got her looks from her father. He was ugly too. My GOD he was ugly, but I loved him. I prayed every day for her to grow up pretty, and you know what? The Lord answered my prayers, because she grew to be the most beautiful young woman I have ever seen."

Regina takes another sip from her wine glass, pulls out a picture of Juliandra's father, and hands it to Thomas.

"This is Reggie, Reggie Washington, Juliandra's father. Despite being ugly, he was a good man; yes he was. Not very good looking, but a good man. Troubled too; oh my lord that man was something else. He was mysterious and the unknown was attractive and I..."

Brighten finally speaks up, "What do you mean troubled mom?"

Before answering, Regina takes two more sips from her glass then refills it again. Brighten moves the almost empty bottle away from her.

"Mom, that's enough wine. You've had enough, alright..."

"Boy, I am a grown ass woman, and I will drink what I want whenever I want, and how much I want."

She puts her glass down on the coffee table and pulls out another picture of Reggie from the photo album.

"Brighten, your father died much too young. He was only 38 when the accident took his life. He never really had the chance to enjoy himself because he always carried a deep pain around. And, he never told anyone about his pain, not even me, and that held him back."

"What are you talking about, mom? What pain?"

"I still don't know what it was he kept secret all his life because he never got a chance to tell me. He died before telling me."

"What?" Brighten asks, "You never found out?"

"Nope, I had to take care of you and your sister, and we had to move on."

"Do you have a computer, Regina?" Thomas asks. "I'd like to do some research."

"No, I don't, but Brighten has a note top thing in his room."

"You mean notebook," Brighten says.

"Yeah notebook... Brighten, let Thomas use your notebook."

Brighten looks over at Thomas, raises an eyebrow, and tells him to go to the kitchen. He gets up, walks off into his room then comes back out, places the notebook on the kitchen table and sits down in front of it.

"Well, what do you wanna research?" Brighten asks.

Thomas sighs, "I'm not sure, I was just going to try and find some clues. Maybe see if anyone who's been to the rehab center was connected with crime."

Brighten opens a web browser. "Got any names, Detective Lee? Perhaps we should type my name in here and see if I'm connected to any big crimes. Maybe, my father was a big criminal too. Yeah, let's see if he was."

Thomas shakes his head as Brighten types REGGIE ALFRED WASHINGTON into the search box then hits the enter key. The search results come up and the third one down is a link to Reggie Washington's obituary.

"Ohh look! There it is... my dad's obituary. Maybe, it was written by drug dealers, or gangsters."

Thomas, sick and tired of Brighten's attitude, starts to walk away.

Suddenly, Brighten calls out. "What's this?"

Thomas stops, walks back to the table, and leans towards the screen. It was an article about a man who was fired from Riverview University. Brighten reads aloud:

"Professor Ronald Ledger loses his tenure after an adopted child comes forward, as an adult, to report past sexual abuse. Reggie Alfred Washington, who was adopted by Professor Ronald Ledger at the age of 7, claimed the abuse began when he turned 9, and continued until he was 16.

Although the Professor was not prosecuted for the alleged crime of sexual assault and sexual abuse of a minor, the University chose to end his tenure.

Ronald Ledger, ultimately, committed suicide after a short life of seclusion and what he described in his suicide note as a loss of respect from his family, and the community."

"Wow!" Thomas says. "I am so sorry Brighten."

Brighten turns to Thomas.

"All this time and all we had to do was just type his name in a little box. Just type his name… and there it is, right in your face."

Thomas leans over again to read the screen as Brighten walks back towards the table.

"They got a picture of that mother fucker?" Brighten asks. "I bet he's white. I bet that abusive ass bitch was white. I hope that son of bitch died slow. I hope he fucked up and did it wrong so he died so slow it lasted all day."

Thomas points at a link to Ronald Ledger's obituary then walks off towards the living room mumbling.

"You know, not all white people are out to get you."

Brighten sits down in front of the computer.

"Oh, don't leave now, Thomas. Come back in here. Let's see what color he is."

Brighten clicks the obituary link.

"I knew it! I knew that motherfucker was white! Thomas, come see! Shit! Shit... Shit... Shit!"

Thomas makes his way back in, "What now? Did you find another white person holding someone down on the internet?"

"Thomas, what is the date right there?"

Thomas squints a bit and moves his head closer to the screen.

"Date of death, July 12th 2001." His eyes widen as he turns toward Brighten. "Today is July 12th!"

"I know today is July 12th. Do you think I would have brought attention to it otherwise?"

"We've gotta call Detective Davis right now. Do you have a phone?"

Brighten hands him a flip phone pulled from his front pocket.

"You trust me with your phone?" Thomas asks.

"Yeah, that phone's a piece of crap. So, yeah, you can use it."

Thomas gets the card Detective Davis gave him, looks for the number and dials it. Three rings and an answer.

"Detective Davis," the voice says.

"Detective, this is Thomas Lee."

"Yes, Mr. Lee, is everything okay?"

"Yeah, we're fine but we found something, something important."

"And what's that?"

"The date... today's date."

"What about the date, Mr. Lee?"

"It matches the date that some professor, named Ronald Ledger, killed himself back in 2001. July 12th 2001!"

"Yes, I know Mr. Lee. I'm checking into that right now. We're looking at all the family members' past histories, but so far we haven't connected the death of Ronald Ledger to this case. He committed suicide, and as far as we can tell it has nothing to do with Juliandra's death other than the date."

"It's gotta have something to do with it." Thomas says. "It can't be a coincidence."

"As of right now, Mr. Lee, it's nothing but a coincidence. Until we can prove otherwise that date is meaningless. I'll look into it further and let you know if we get any relevant information, okay?"

"Alright, Detective."

"Hold on a second, Mr. Lee, there's something here that's concerning to me."

"What is it?" Thomas replies.

"I'm looking at the death certificate for Ronald Ledger and the time of death is 9:36am. As I recall you claimed that someone was going to shoot Juliandra at 9:36 this morning."

For a moment, Thomas is speechless and takes a few seconds to respond.

"Yes, that was the time they said it would happen."

"Okay, I want you to hang tight while I make some calls, alright? I'll call you back once we have more details."

"Yes, okay, bye."

The detective hangs up with no further response. Brighten, waiting for answers at the table, is looking straight at Thomas.

"Well?" he asks.

"The time matched," Thomas says.

"The time?"

"On the death certificate for the professor, his time of death was 9:36am."

"Excuse me? What?"

"9:36am. That's when Juliandra was shot this morning. 9:36 A-fuckin'-M! Something to do with this professor got Juliandra killed today. I'm callin' his wife."

"Whose wife?"

"Ronald Ledger's wife. I wanna talk to her and find out what the hell her husband had to do with this. She has to know something."

"Don't you think the Detective is gonna call her? It's his job man. He already knew about this professor. He's probably talking to the bitch right now."

"Maybe, but I need to make sure. I need to know what this guy has to do with all of this. Come on man; let me use your computer so I can at least **do** something."

"Have at it. I... am going to wake my mom and tell her about my father's past. And, if you break my notebook you're buying me a new one."

Brighten walks off into the living room where Regina has fallen asleep with a picture of Reggie and Juliandra still in her hand. Thomas sits in front of the computer and immediately begins putting all his work experience to use. *Its 2014,* he thinks. *Everyone is linked in some way with information stored on servers around the world. I just have to find it.*

After bouncing from page to page for fifteen minutes Thomas runs across a second obituary for Ronald Ledger. A quick read reveals that it's mostly identical to the first except one subtle difference. He reads part of it out loud.

"He is survived by his wife Patricia Ledger, his stepson Jeremy Miles..."

The first obituary hadn't said anything about a stepson, and further research uncovers that Jeremy had committed suicide on July 12th 2004, having never started a family of his own.

How odd, Thomas thinks. *Suicide on the same day your step dad kills himself? And why Juliandra on that same day? What the hell does she have to do with any of this?*

Thomas immediately begins searching for a way to contact Ronald Ledger's widow Patricia. In his mind, he must speak with her. She must know the link. He, reluctantly, calls for Brighten who's still on the couch with his mother talking. After ten minutes of back and forth, Thomas convinces Brighten to let him use a credit card to acquire contact information on Patricia Ledger who is currently living in Boston. Thomas gets a phone number and without hesitation dials it with Brighten beside him.

A man's voice answers: "Hello?"

Thomas hesitates for a moment before speaking. "Is this the residence of Patricia Ledger?"

"Yes," the voice replies.

"I need to speak with Mrs. Ledger, please."

"I'm sorry, but she's not here at the moment. May I leave a message for her, sir?"

"When will she return?"

"She may return in an hour, tonight, or tomorrow. I have no idea, sir. May I leave a message for you?"

"Is there any way I can get ahold of her now? Can you find her? Where is she?"

"Listen, sir, I don't know who you are, but if you need to talk to her, she will be back sometime today or tomorrow. Now, you can leave a message or you can hang up; your choice."

Thomas paces back and forth a few seconds thinking how to respond.

"You listen," he says to the man, "I am Detective Lee from the Bangor P.D. and I need to speak with her now."

Brighten looks at Thomas with a surprised expression then moves his lips silently as if to say, *"what?!"*

"Look Detective Lee," the man says. "Detective Davis already called here, and I gave him her cellphone number. That's all I can do. Okay?"

"Yes, Detective Davis and I are working on a case together, but he hasn't checked in yet. Can you please give me that number again, so I can make a note of it?"

"Well, whatever you two *"detectives"* are working on, I hope it's not too important, because if you can't keep track of a phone number, you have no hope to solve anything."

"Sir, can you just give me the number?"

"Alright, but if a third *"detective"* calls here from your department, they're getting nothing, damn incompetent fools. Hold on... 6175554387, you got that?"

"Yes, I have it. Thank you sir, have a nice day."

"Uh huh," replies the man before disconnecting.

Thomas dials the number he just obtained for Patricia Ledger.

"Wow!" He says. "What an asshole that guy was! Oh, it's ringing."

"Yes?" A voice answers.

"Hello, Mrs. Ledger?"

"Yes."

"This is Detective Lee from the Bangor P.D. I was hoping you could answer a few questions for me."

"Are you serious? I just got off the phone with Detective Davis; I'm not going over everything again."

Thomas starts to pace around again and then stops.

"No, no ma'am, just a couple of follow up questions, I assure you."

"What more could you possibly need to know?" she asks. "My husband was a child molester who turned my son gay then killed himself. That's it. That's the story. I gave Detective Davis all the details."

"Ahh yes, but we are... we are concerned about the date of your son's death."

"Yes, I told your partner already. Jeremy was obsessed with Ronald, and in some weird act of honor or some crap like that killed himself on the anniversary of Ronald's suicide. We've been through all this. Jeremy wouldn't talk to me after his stepfather died, and the only one he did talk to was his friend Jason."

"Jason?"

"Yes, I think he was gay, and he and his little art collecting butt buddy did everything together. Jason Brean and him were lovers I think. That's all I know."

"Do you have a number for Jason, Mrs. Ledger?"

"No, I don't. I didn't want to know him, and I don't care. All I know is he lives somewhere near the Bristoly Lounge. That's where those two always went. Now... are we done? I'm tired of talking about this, and I'm very busy."

"Yes, Mrs. Ledger, yes. Thank you very much, and I'm sorry."

Mrs. Ledger ends the call abruptly.

"Boy..." Brighten says. "You are crazy with that lying shit. I am impressed man. I cannot believe you pulled that shit off."

Thomas smiles. "It's the way hackers get information," he says. "Many of them pose as someone they're not to con people out of account information. I just thought like a hacker."

"You know what that is? That's a white person thing man. You don't see many black people hacking do you? White people are doin' all that shit."

Thomas's smile quickly changes to a frown as he shakes his head.

"You know Brighten, come to think of it, you're right. I have never seen a hacker that's black."

"Exactly! Now you're seeing things, Thomas. There's hope for you yet."

"But," Thomas replies, "that may mean they're just not getting caught as much as the white guys."

Thomas sits back down at the table in front of the computer and begins to search for information about Jason Brean. *This one's alive at least,* he thinks. After finding some details on the man, he tries several phone numbers. Each leads to a dead end, disconnected number, or 'no longer in service' message.

"I know this guy has a phone; I mean, who doesn't today? It's unlisted or something."

"Or..." Brighten says. "He switched to some kind of prepaid phone. I have a friend that calls me every other week with a new phone number. He just gets a new phone when he can afford it."

"I need my wallet," Thomas says.

"What? Why?"

"I'm gonna find this guy in Boston. He knows something and I don't have time to wait for Detective Davis."

"Ohh contraire. That is all you have. We... are gonna stay right here until the police say otherwise."

Thomas looks over at a clock in the kitchen, covertly picks up the credit card Brighten let him use and without a word walks to the bathroom and shuts the door. He sees that the window is big enough to fit through and climbs out.

CHAPTER 8 - THE ANSWERS

It takes an hour and a half for Thomas to get to Rosewater Avenue where law enforcement remains present working around his home. The police cruiser, Juliandra died in, is still parked in front, and now has red colored sticks protruding from it, depicting the trajectory of each bullet. All Thomas needs is his wallet, which should be in the bedroom on the nightstand. Quietly, he maneuvers himself to the back yard and waits for an opportunity to get inside without being seen.

It was warm last night and they had left one bedroom window open, but the trick will be getting the screen off and climbing in unnoticed. He crawls around looking for something, anything to help pry the screen out. During the search Thomas stops and shakes his head. *What am I doing?* He thinks. *My belt buckle... Duh!* Thomas moves back to the window, removes his belt, and uses the buckle's prong like a screwdriver to pry the lower part of the screen upward. Slowly, he pulls it out and sets it on the ground. From the outside the bottom of the window is as high as his shoulders, creating a need to have at least a small object to stand on in order to get in quietly. This problem is quickly resolved when he grabs one of Juliandra's potted plants, empties it out, and flips it upside down to use as a step.

Once inside, Thomas crouches and looks over at the nightstand, but doesn't see the wallet. He drops to his hands and knees and begins to search in all directions, thinking he might have moved it during the mornings' events. Clearly, it wasn't in the bedroom, so he slowly crawls out into the living room, making sure to stay below the windows. Just as he peaks over toward a table holding the entire weeks worth of mail, two voices from outside become clear and begin to get louder as if a couple of policemen were walking towards the open window. Thomas freezes in place and turns his head in that direction to see if anyone comes in to view.

What seemed to be an extraordinary amount of time to stay in one spot, remaining absolutely motionless, soon pays off. Those voices that had become loud and clear begin to get further and further away, easing his tension and allowing him to turn back toward the table in the entryway. There it was on the floor, underneath, where it must have fallen. Without pause, he shimmies across the floor and grabs the wallet before turning to make the short but nerve-racking journey into the bedroom where the open window awaited his departure.

The distant voices start getting louder again as Thomas slowly makes headway on his trek to get out of the house. He could easily make out the conversation. It was two officers walking the perimeter using some optical equipment to measure distance at various points. Again he has to pause for a few moments before the voices travel away, giving him another opportunity to act and escape the potential of getting caught inside. Moving as silently as possible he climbs out and sneaks his way to the property line, leaving the scene on foot. *Holy crap, I can't take much more of this.*

While walking, the mission becomes clear, and his thoughts focused. He's going to rent a car and head to Boston to find Jason. Time is of the essence and he's got to avoid sleep at all cost, or he'll have to relive the morning's events all over. In his travels he spots a small BMX style bicycle in someone's yard. *It's not right to just take it,* he thinks. *But, I believe the owner would understand.* A quick look around and the bike becomes his current mode of transportation.

It takes some time, but he finally arrives near the airport, drops the bike, and walks the rest of the way. Wallet in hand, Thomas steps into the rental office and in no time drives out of the parking lot with a minivan. The van seemed a better choice since there was no way of knowing what might be needed later. So many theories, plans, ideas and random thoughts keep zipping around in his mind. *Should I have a weapon? Poor Reggie. How do I act? Who do I say I am? Life seems meaningless without her. What if this guy can't be found? What if I find him? This is all crazy!*

The first stop is at a nearby SuperStore to grab food, a change of clothes, and energy drinks that will undoubtedly become one of the essential weapons against his body's desire to nod off. It takes almost 45 minutes to pick out supplies, pay, and make it back to the vehicle before getting on the road. According to the GPS, it'll be another three hours and forty-six minutes before arriving at the Bristoly Lounge where Jeremy and Jason spent so much time. It's a long shot, but Thomas is determined to do something rather than wait.

The sun's going down, the night's closing in, and his long trip comes to an end when the van stops right in front of the building's main entrance. It was the second closest parking spot there, and he couldn't help but feel that under any other circumstances it would have been impossible to get. *It was Saturday night, a good night to go out,* he thinks, *the odds could work.* Trying to be discrete, Thomas quickly swaps his clothes inside the van then heads into the building through the double doors. The lounge is to the left and now all he has to do is go in and wait to see if Jason shows up. It only takes 12 steps to find a chair and only 10 seconds to notice someone at the bar who resembles the picture of Jason he saw online. *Plan...*

plan...plan... I need a plan, Thomas is frantically thinking. *Art... I'm into art, and I am interested in buying some art. That's it.*

Unsure but anxious, tentative but motivated, he rises out of his seat and walks towards the bar while trying to force himself to relax. His hands are sweaty and slightly shaking as he approaches. The gentleman, who's waiting for a drink, happens to turn and makes eye contact. *Nope, not him,* Thomas thinks as he veers off to the right side of the bar.

"I'll be with you in a moment." The bartender says.

"I'm in no hurry," Thomas replies. "I'm just waiting for a friend anyway."

The bartender pours the contents of a shaker into a glass, pushes it towards a gentleman in front of him then walks over to Thomas.

"What can I get for you?"

"Well, I don't want to start drinking without my friend." Thomas explains. "Can I get a club soda with cranberry juice for now?"

The bartender grabs a glass and fills it with ice. "No problem at all," he says. "First time in the lounge?"

"Yes actually, I've never been here, but it's really nice."

"It can be. I guess it depends on who comes in. I've been around quite some time and people always seem to find themselves in chaotic situations, even though they're a tiny bit more civilized these days."

"Hah... Very true, they are just a tiny bit more civilized. Not much though. I think the surroundings have changed but people haven't"

"You have no idea how right you are. But, that's a whole other story. So, did your friend recommend the lounge? Have they been here before?"

"Yes, he did. He comes here all the time and never stops talking about you. I mean you guys. Well, I mean the lounge and the staff of course."

The bartender hands Thomas his drink. "Really? I know a few of the regulars. What's his name?"

"Jason."

"Hmmm, I see a couple Jasons in here often... Common name though; what's his last name? I know a Jason Morellow and a Jason Brean."

"Jason Brean! That's him," Thomas says. "That's my friend."

"Ohh yeah, he's here quite a bit. In fact, he stays at the hotel almost every Friday and Saturday. Seems like a decent guy; talks about painting and photography all the time. Thought I saw him earlier. He may have beaten ya here."

"No Way."

"Yeah, let's see. Try over to the right side. I think he's at a booth with another friend of yours."

"Hey, thanks. I'll go find him. Thanks again."

A sudden shower of nerves falls over Thomas as he walks off. After all, he's moving in the direction of a man who could potentially shed some light on his now dark life. A few steps and there he is, sitting alone sipping from a wine glass. On the opposite side of his table sat another glass, empty and abandoned. Thomas slows his pace long enough to confirm it's actually Jason and then continues to approach while forcing his lips to smile. Several thoughts about how to ask questions swirl through his head as he gets closer and closer. The pace slows again as the details of Jason's face become clear. He can see tears making their way down his cheeks. Suddenly, out of the blue, that unoccupied seat across from the crying man gets refilled as a forty something year old guy, in a black pinstripe suite, sits down. Thomas quickly chooses an open table nearby and plunks down. Jason is clearly upset and talking loudly to the person in front of him. Thomas sits patiently; nursing his drink and trying listen without looking directly at them for too long. Unexpectedly, a lounge server pops into his view and asks if he'd like to see a menu.

It startled him, but he thought, *how Perfect. Of course, that will buy me some time.*

"Yes, please," he replies. "I'd love a menu."

The server fades from his vision as quickly as she appeared and Thomas focuses his hearing on the conversation that is now privy to anyone within a 30-foot radius. He can hear Jason loud and clear.

"Today is the anniversary of Jeremy," he says before getting hushed by his associate.

Jason's voice lowers as he wipes a tear from his right eye and mumbles something to the other man whom he's called Chief twice. It takes Thomas a minute to process what he heard, but he believes he understood him to say, "That fuckin' bitch's father might as well have killed him."

This Chief guy hushes him again, gets up and leaves the lounge angry. He isn't the only one angry at this point. Thomas is filling with rage and he doesn't even know the context of their conversation. It's been too much today; too much has happened and he just wants answers. That statement has to be what he thought; it has to be. Thomas orders a burger to waste time and watches Jason as he continues to drink. A change of plan is needed. Asking questions is no good anymore. It has to be an interrogation. He has to get him alone.

A few more drinks and the server taking care of Jason's table decides to cut him off, and informs him that the lounge will not bring anymore alcoholic beverages. Jason becomes loud, belligerent, and begins to cause a scene. He demands another drink and starts a long streak of cursing, calling the server several names and commenting on how useless she is. The lady stayed calm and collected, explaining again that they can't serve him anymore, and if he doesn't calm down they'll have him escorted out. Jason stands up, starts to walk, but trips over his own feet and falls to the ground. *Karma!* Thomas thinks. *And, opportunity.* He springs up and walks over to Jason who's trying his best to push off the floor and onto his knees. Thomas extends his arm and reaches for Jason's hand to help.

"It's okay ma'am, I got him. My friend here is just upset tonight. I'll help him out."

Jason looks at the server. "Yeah, my friend here is gonna help me out lady. Not you or your stupid ass lounge police. Oooohhh."

Jason reaches in his right pocket, pulls out the contents and sifts through it to find two one hundred dollar bills which he tosses onto the table. Something in the mix of paper and money catches Thomas's eye. It was a small picture. It was Brighten. He couldn't believe what it was, but it was there. Jason crumbles everything back up, shoves it into his pocket and starts to stagger away. Thomas is enraged, but does his best to smile while following Jason out of the lounge area and into the hotel lobby. Jason steps towards the elevators and reaches in his pocket again, looking for his room key. The plastic key falls to the floor and Thomas leans down to reach for it. He makes out the room number 612 written on the sleeve just before Jason snatches it away and continues toward the elevators. Thomas follows until Jason stops and turns around.

"This is where we part ways friend, unless you're coming up to my room to blow me." He laughs a bit, "Understand?"

Thomas raises his hands to gesture his understanding and doesn't take another step as Jason enters one of the elevators. As soon as the doors close he makes his way to the stairway and runs up to the sixth floor as fast as he can. Out of breath and dripping sweat, he completes the last set of stairs and pushes open the metal door to find he's made it just as Jason is walking out of the elevator. Thomas stays by the doorway and waits to see which direction he will go. Nobody else is around, but thinking it looks suspicious to be standing in one place, he decides to walk casually in the direction of Jason. Thomas stays a few steps behind until Jason gets his door open. When it widens enough, he speeds up and pushes him inside, not even thinking about who or what could be in there. Once again, the tearful yet belligerent drunk man ends up on the floor after losing his footing from the sudden accelerated entry to his room.

"What the fuck man?" Jason slurs as he rolls over to see who pushed him. "What the fuck? Ohh, it's you friend. Come to suck my dick I see. Well get to it! Ahh hahaha, all you had to do was ask."

Thomas, still enraged at the mere thought of Jason's involvement, shuts the room door and steps over his body to deliver multiple punches to his jaw, knocking him out. It was disturbing to him how easily the man on the floor lost consciousness. *How fragile*, he thought. *One second a man is talking and the next second he might as well not exist.* The idea was scary. Anger and regret are mixed together with feelings of sympathy now that the loud obnoxious voice is silent. Anger does seem to be the strongest though.

"Suck that, you piss ant." He says under his breath.

Thomas removes everything from Jason's pockets and searches through the contents before scrambling to prop him up into an office chair at a small desk. He uses the power cords from the hotel hair dryer and coffee maker to tie the man's legs and hands together before grabbing a clothes iron from the closet and rolling the chair into the bathroom. Jason is slowly gaining consciousness, and soon his eyes open and begin to shift left then right before homing in on Thomas who's standing directly in front of him, staring at a picture. In one hand he's holding a pile of papers mixed with money and a photo of Brighten. In the other, an image of Juliandra extracted from that pile. Jason begins to scream, yelling out for help. Thomas puts the picture in his pocket and proceeds to punch Jason in the nose.

"Stop screaming or I'll punch you until you have no face. Stop screaming," Thomas says.

Blood pours from Jason's nose and falls over his lips down his chin, mixing with the steady stream of uncontrollable tears from his eyes. He begins to spit onto the floor in an effort to keep the fluid from building up and sticking to his mouth. Thomas knows that this is the guy, this is the man with the answers, and he can't, he won't, he must not stop until he gets those answers. He grabs the iron and plugs it in to a power outlet, turning the dial to the highest setting.

"I just wanna say that I've seen a lot of movies, and I'm pretty sure I can torture the living hell out of you if I need to. In fact, my favorite movie has a scene where this guy takes a hot iron and burns the crap out of the bad guy until he tells him what he wants to know. Have you ever seen that movie? It's got the best torture scene ever, the best in my opinion anyway. I mean, I don't have an iron. Ohh... Wait, I do have this iron here. And look, it's heating up right now."

"What the hell do you want friend?" Jason asks.

"I want some questions answered. I'm not a violent man, but I'll do what I have to if you don't answer my questions."

"Who do you think you are? Are you some kind of cop or something?"

"Who am I? Who do I think I am?" Thomas says. "How about who was I? You fuck! I was a husband, and I was a happy man, and I was someone enjoying life until this morning."

"What are you talking about?"

"I... am talking about my wife, Juliandra. How about, who was Juliandra? Huh!"

Jason's eyes widen for just a second, giving away his familiarity with Juliandra's name. "Who is Juliandra?" He asks.

Thomas immediately punches Jason in the nose again. "Wrong answer. Try again!"

He reaches back to the iron, taps the bottom to test the temperature and picks it up.

"I want to know how you're connected with my wife's death."

Jason spits a bit of blood onto the floor. "I don't know what the hell you're talking about," he says.

Thomas closes his eyes for a few seconds before reaching back to throw another fist. Jason suddenly lunges upward and grabs Thomas with a loud grunt. The power cord binding his wrists didn't hold well, and he was able to loosen it enough to free his hands. The hot iron slides into the sink and the two men slam against the bathroom door. Out of instinct, from repetitive training during taekwondo classes, Thomas clasps his hands behind Jason's neck and drives his right knee into him over and over until Jason collapses to the floor. Thomas picks him up, throws him back into the chair, grabs the lose power cord and reties his wrists as tight as possible with no regard for blood flow. He steps toward the sink still breathing heavily, looks into the mirror and sees a man who is desperate, angry, and losing his moral bearings. *Focus...* he thinks *Focus!* Jason is also breathing heavily, starts coughing, and eventually vomits onto the floor and his own body.

"Tell me what I need to know and I won't hurt you anymore," Thomas says.

"I don't know anything."

Thomas grabs the hot iron and hovers it over Jason's left thigh. A tear falls from his face as speaks again. "Tell me what you know about my wife, Juliandra."

"I don't know her." Jason replies.

An ear piercing scream envelops the room as Thomas presses the iron down and holds it. Smoke begins to billow upward followed by a faint sizzling sound and the smell of burning flesh. Thomas pulls it off, puts the iron back in the sink, and ties a towel around Jason's mouth to keep him quiet.

"Just let me know when you want to talk, alright? I'm going to move the iron to a different part of your body until there's nowhere left to burn."

Thomas reaches again for the iron and presses it against Jason's right thigh, holding it in place while Jason screams into the towel.

"Just let me know when you have some answers." He says.

60 seconds go by before he pulls the iron off, moves it to Jason's chest and pushes it forward; holding it there until he can no longer stand the sound of Jason's muffled screams or the smell of his skin burning. Thomas backs away, puts the iron down and leans into the bathtub just in time to vomit while Jason remains bound wincing in pain and shaking his head back and forth. He turns the shower on to mask the noises and wash away the mess, picks up the iron, and starts again. From outside the bathroom door the sound of spraying water and muffled screams fill the room for over ten minutes before nothing but the sound of the shower remains. The screams were replaced by a pain filled voice, the volume of which would change in cycles as Jason's brain registered the magnitude of his burns.

Thirty more minutes pass before Thomas finally comes out and closes the door behind him. Jason talked. He finally broke and told Thomas everything he wanted to know. Thomas had succeeded, but it didn't feel like success at all. It felt empty, unsatisfying, and wrong. *Do the ends really justify the means?* He thought. He didn't know anymore but the answers were brought to light.

It was all for Jeremy who Jason had been in love with for many years. He explained that Professor Ledger sexually abused both Reggie and Jeremy, but Jeremy had developed some kind of twisted bond with the Professor, who was also his stepfather. He felt the abuse was out of love, a way in which his stepfather expressed how much he cared. Jeremy became jealous of Reggie for receiving extra attention and developed a deep hatred for him later after he accused the Professor of sexual abuse. Eventually, his stepfather committed suicide and Jeremy vowed revenge for his loss. He paid to have Reggie killed, but that death didn't make him feel better for long. He wanted Reggie's family to suffer even more. He wanted them to feel the loss that he felt. After living three years without his stepfather, he couldn't bare it anymore and committed suicide himself on the third anniversary of Ronald Ledger's death.

In a final act of vengeance, just before Jeremy ended his own life, he asked Jason to hire three separate assassins to shoot one of Reggie's children on the tenth anniversary of his death, July 12th 2014. The three contracted killers were instructed to fire only once so there would be three bullets in the victim, one for each year Jeremy was alive without the love of his stepfather. It was his ultimate revenge and was to be done at exactly 9:36am, Ronald Ledger's time of death. Thomas almost felt sorry for Jason as he was telling the story. Jason loved Jeremy enough to kill for him ten years after he was dead, even though Jeremy had only ever really loved his stepfather. In some strange way, Thomas couldn't help but respect Jason for holding out so long during the interrogation. That feeling however was short lived once he learned it was a mere coin toss that decided Juliandra's fate. Nothing more than a damn coin toss. Jason didn't care which one died, only that the person he had once loved asked him to do it.

Thomas walks over to the bed, sits, and begins to cry. It was all too much to take in. He can't believe what he has done to another human being for the sake of his own cause. *Was it just? Was he right? Does this end justify his means?* He looks up into a mirror on the wall, wipes away the tears then pulls the picture of Juliandra from his pocket.

Yes… For now, the answer is yes.

CHAPTER 9 - THE WAIT

A plethora of information has bombarded Thomas and caused him to struggle with sorting out what to focus on first. It takes a while, but eventually the path to his next move starts to clear. He knows the man named Chief was just in the lounge and has plans to catch a flight to Las Vegas tomorrow morning. It's also still relatively early, and now, seems as good a time as any to try and nab him. Thomas walks back into the bathroom and closes the door. A few minutes later he comes out and heads directly to the room's desk, opens the topside drawer, then pulls out a small bag containing a prepaid cell phone. It was the phone Jason had used to communicate with all three of Juliandra's killers, and had used over the past month. Its fate had also been predetermined since it was going to be destroyed once all contracts were paid in full.

Thomas writes the number on a piece of paper along with other information that could help him save Juliandra's life. He starts to read it all out loud saying it over and over trying to memorize as much as possible. It was all-important, and he'd done everything he could up to this point. He needed more, more details. He needed to interrogate one of the killers. *Enough!* he thinks. *I've got to question Chief.* Thomas heads back into the bathroom with the phone and commands Jason to call the man, referred to as Chief, in an effort to get him back to the hotel. At first, Jason refuses, explaining that Chief has already been paid and doesn't have any reason to return, but it only takes a quick reminder of how much more pain could be inflicted to get him to agree. Jason's tune changes and he tells Thomas that Chief might be convinced to come back by the interest of a new job. Thomas dials the number and holds the phone as Jason encourages the man on the other end to pay him a visit as soon as possible. The call ends. It was done and the wait begins.

The question is... Would the man indeed show up thinking there is another high paying contract on the table? Thomas exits the bathroom and begins pacing the floor trying to memorize everything he can, including the phone numbers used by the three shooters Jason identified as Chief, Roy, and Boon. The wait seems forever, and his thoughts continually drift between numbers and questions. Without warning, the main door opens, and a man walks straight in carrying his own room key. Thomas is taken off guard and freezes in place. The man calmly shuts the door then reaches inside his suite jacket and pulls out a small-framed pistol which he points in Thomas's direction.

"Where's Jason?" He asks.

Although completely still, Thomas's mind is engaged at Mach 3 trying to calculate the next move, the next step, the way he will avoid being killed.

"Jason's in the bathroom puking his ass off from drinking too much," Thomas replies. "He's kind of a pussy, actually."

It was him, the man who sat with Jason in the lounge, the one known as Chief. Groans of pain emanate from the bathroom and the armed man smiles. He turns slightly and reaches for the door, opens it, and looks inside. As the killer makes his visual inspection Thomas becomes more desperate, glancing around trying to come up with a way out of the situation. *It's all over,* he thinks. *It's going to end right here. I can't let it end here.*

"You're right, he is a pussy." Chief says. "Did you do that to him?"

"Yeah, I had to find you," Thomas replies. "I'm desperate to have someone... Well... Taken out, and Jason wouldn't tell me how to get ahold of his best man."

After speaking, Thomas feels immediate regret for every word he uttered. *That was stupid! FUCK! It's done now.*

Chief takes a step forward. "Now that you found me the results may not be what you expect, mister."

He then reaches with his left hand into his right jacket pocket and pulls out a black cylinder. *Alright, it's definitely over anyway,* Thomas thinks, *Nothing to lose, nothing at all.* Chief holds the cylinder up and begins to twist it onto the front of the guns barrel. Thomas mumbles, "Fuck it!" and sprints toward the weapon as fast as he can. He reaches out with his left hand open and pushes the gun away before tightening his grip and prying it from Chief's hand. It was a technique he'd tried during self-defense training but never really thought would work in real life.

Adrenaline still at max, Thomas takes a quick glance at the gun in his hand and says, "Holy shit!" out loud. He doesn't pause for long though and quickly pushes Chief backwards with his left foot, immediately spins right, and strikes the hired gun with a back kick, knocking him to the floor. It was imperative that he disable Chief to keep him under control, so Thomas runs forward and drives his right knee into the man's face as he tries to get up, and then uses the bottom of the gun to strike his temple continuously until all signs of consciousness are gone. He had to pause for a second; he was simply amazed that his quick action completely flipped the situation around. *Wow! Fuck, shit, shit, holy shit! I can't believe that just happened. Fuck! I've got to tie this guy up quick!*

He knows that within seconds this terrible person will wake up and start screaming or struggling. There's no choice, he's got to do something fast. Thomas runs over to the desk and puts the gun in the top left drawer before rushing back to Chief. Thomas picks up Chief's right arm, holds it in a large joint lock and uses leverage to bend it at the elbow until it hyper extends backwards, breaking the joint and rendering the arm unusable. He repeats the process to the left arm to make sure there will be no struggle when he comes to. Just as he reaches out and grabs the legs with the intention of dragging him into the bathroom, he stops to think. *I've got to prevent this guy from doing anything at all. I can't risk him trying to get away or trying to fight. His knees!*

Thomas immediately reaches down and grabs the gunman's right ankle, pulls it up, and begins to force his elbow down onto the knee trying to hyper extend the joint. It wasn't working; he couldn't get enough leverage and time was running out. Next, he steps over the knee facing the foot, squats down and clasps the ankle with both hands. In a quick motion he pulls upward on the leg while dropping his body weight down on the knee causing it to snap. It was a horrible sound, much worse than the elbows. It was almost impossible to avoid vomiting. *One down one more to go. Better make damn sure.* Reluctantly, Thomas steps over the left knee and repeats the process.

"Now that fuck is going nowhere," he says out loud.

Suddenly, his gag reflex gains strength and he's forced to grab the small trash can near the desk in order to expel the last of his stomach's contents. The more he released the more he gagged and the more he gagged the more he spewed. Finally, it was enough, and it didn't take long to recollect his thoughts and focus. He had to get Chief into the bathroom before he woke up. Thomas quickly searches through every pocket on Chief's clothing and removes all the items, placing them on a small tray found earlier by the coffee maker. He then drags him into the bathroom.

"Hey Jason, your friend is here!"

Now, Chief's nightmare begins as the water from the shower slams down onto his face, and he's thrust into the awareness of his injuries.

"Ahhh, what have you done to me? My fuckin' arms! Ahhh, I can't... My legs! What the hell? What do you want from me?"

"Chief," Thomas says, "I don't have much time because I need to find your buddy Roy before he disappears. I'm sorry about your arms and your legs. I had to make sure you wouldn't cause me any trouble when you woke up. Wait, no... Come to think of it, I don't believe I am sorry about it. See, you shot my wife this morning, and well, that wasn't a good thing to do."

"I don't know what you're talking about mister. I didn't shoot anybody."

"Ohh, this game again, huh? I don't understand why everyone lies. Why don't you just tell the truth right away and avoid getting tortured? I don't get it; do you Jason? Well, let's ask Jason about it, shall we. So Jason, is this Chief? Is this one of the men you hired to kill my wife?"

Thomas looks over and sees him nodding his head ever so slightly.

"You see, Chief, or whatever the hell your name is, Jason has come to grips with the truth and he says you're one of the **FUCKS** I'm looking for, and guess what? I believe him. I do, 'cuz

120

Jason and I have an understanding now. Hell, we could be friends if he hadn't hired three killers to shoot my wife!"

Thomas reaches over towards the iron sitting on the countertop still plugged in and turns the heat dial to linen. Without pause he leans over the tub, grabs Chief and pulls him out, slamming him onto the tile floor.

"I have a few questions for you, CHIEF! And, if you don't answer them, I'm gonna make you look worse than Jason."

Chief, immediately, cries out, "Okay, okay! What do you want to know? What? What?"

"Well, where were you this morning when you pulled the trigger? Where *exactly*, were you?"

"Why does it matter? I did it. I did it. Just turn me in, for God sakes."

Thomas reaches for the iron, takes Chief's right hand and flips it so the palm is up. He presses the iron down onto it as hard as he can for a count of ten while covering Chief's mouth with a hand towel.

"The next time I ask a question, you just answer it, or this iron will be on your fucking face! Do you understand me? Do you understand me?"

Chief is groaning, pleading for mercy, "Yes, yes, I was in a house 250 yards from your home. The owner was on vacation, so I used it."

"What house? What was the address? And, I want to know what room you were in and what direction you were looking."

"2499 Rosewater Avenue," he says, "just up the hill from your house on the opposite side of the street. I was in the southwest corner, in the bedroom facing down the hill at your house."

"Wait, wait a second. Did you move at any time? I mean, you were going to shoot her in the kitchen and then you shot her in the police car. Did you have to move?"

"What? No, I had a clear shot of the kitchen and the driveway. How the hell did you know we intended to drop her in the kitchen?"

Thomas grabs the iron and moves it towards Chief's face. "I told you to answer the damn questions not ask questions!"

"Alright, alright! I'm sorry, hold on! Wait, wait!"

"So you didn't have to move?"

"No, my view was good, I never had to move."

"The other two, Roy and Boon, where were they to start with? If they were going to shoot into my kitchen."

"I don't know exactly where they were. All I know is that I was to shoot from the North East, Roy from the North and Boon was South West of your house. I swear that's all I know."

"I want to know every detail of what you did from 8:36am to 9:36am. Tell me everything. I want to know what you were doing the whole time, if you went to the bathroom, if you scratched your ass, looked over your shoulder, everything. And, I want to know what you brought with you and where you put it. Guns, knives, two way radio, cellphone; tell me every detail of what you had and where it was."

Chief begins explaining exactly what he had done during that time, minute by minute, while Thomas listens intently, jotting down important details on a hotel notepad. He listens for over an hour as Chief recalls every small element of his movements.

Thomas learns that all three had been instructed not to shoot until 9:36am unless Juliandra was thought to be leaving the home, at which point they were to fire at will. Each gunman was settled in by 8:36am and Juliandra's fate seemed to be sealed. After a while though, Thomas was convinced he could get to Chief's location and neutralize him in less than fifteen minutes. 250 yards wasn't a lot of ground to cover on foot, but it would take more time to cover that distance covertly. He'd also need time to somehow disable Chief before he could pull the trigger.

Thomas creates a drawing of the room Chief described, then makes points on it showing where each item was supposed to be located. It was like having the lottery numbers before they were drawn, except the prize was life not millions of dollars. If he maintains the advantage of surprise and gets to them unnoticed, it would be possible. No, not possible, there could be no conditions, it had to work... it had to. The next step is to question Roy and Boon to find out their exact locations. According to Chief, the three hired guns didn't know each other and shared little information about themselves, just enough to coordinate the job. He only knew Boon came down from Canada, was going to take the longest shot, and Roy was up from Mexico and taking the second longest shot. That was alright though because Thomas had something he could use to find them, Jason.

Thomas stuffs a small hand towel in Chief's mouth and ties another longer one around his face to keep it there.

"Keep your mouth shut" he tells him. "If you make any noise the iron is going to be your lunch."

His focus is back to Jason. Two more murderers had to be tracked down which meant two more calls had to be made, and soon before they destroyed their phones. Surprisingly, Jason offers no resistance this time when he's told to convince Roy and Boon that a meeting is necessary. Thomas almost didn't even have to ask as he held the phone up. Jason was able to persuade Roy to take a meeting at noon in Houlton, Maine, and the man known as Boon the following day in New York City at 10:00am. This would create an incredible challenge for Thomas, as he needed to remain awake the entire time or risk falling asleep and starting all over again. He's was used to working late hours, but had never tried to stay awake for the amount of time it was going to take to finally meet with Boon, and hopefully get the answers he needed. Not only did he have to get those answers but he needed to memorize as much information as possible. As he paced around, he took every opportunity to say out loud the most important details he wanted to remember.

What he needed now was a map to help visualize everything. It would be handy to view the home and its surroundings from above. After tying Chief's broken arms behind his body, tightening the cords that held Jason in place, and doing his best to prevent them from making any sound, Thomas puts the 'do not disturb' sign on the room door and heads down into the hotel lobby to use a guest computer. He brings up a satellite view of his house on a mapping website and looks it over. Zooming out reveals the house Chief was in this morning and sparks the thoughts of where the other two men might have been. He also notices the satellite image is dated 2013, and there were two vehicles being washed in the driveway the day the photo was taken, a small pickup truck and a four door SUV. *I wonder,* he thinks. *What if one of those vehicles was there?*

Thomas moves the map on the screen back to his house and zooms in to get a closer look. Something catches his eye. It was a spot on the roof. Two more clicks to get even closer and he recognizes the object. *My shoe!* In an instant he becomes overwhelmed by the memory of how it got there…

CHAPTER 10 - THE SHOE

It was just getting dark outside. Clouds were forming in the sky while sounds of thunder cracked overhead and echoed for miles. Thomas had cancelled his taekwondo classes and was driving home after finishing a slightly longer day of work. As he pulled into the driveway he noticed Juliandra had not yet made it there and decided to surprise her by making dinner.

Excited and eager to set the tone for the evening, Thomas quickly gathered everything he needed from his truck, went inside the house, and threw his keys onto a small table near the entrance. Wanting to know the time he glanced over at a large clock on the living room wall, remembered how much he hated analog ones then looked at his cell instead. There wasn't much time to cook, so he picked up the pace a bit and started thinking about what to make. Just as he headed into the kitchen, light beamed in through the living room windows, and the sound of an engine got louder and suddenly stopped.

It was Juliandra's car. *Oh yeah,* he thought, *she's usually here about this time, and I'm always late.*

Sure enough, the front door opened and in popped Juliandra. She had a huge smile on her face and two small bags from the China Now restaurant.

"I guessed right," she said. "I thought you'd get here before me so I grabbed us some Chinese food."

Thomas dropped to his knees and put his hands together. "Baby, I love you so much!" he said. "You rock!"

Juliandra walked over, kissed him on the forehead then made her way into the kitchen where she pulled out the food containers and opened them up.

"Here baby, I got you some sesame chicken and steamed rice."

Thomas smiled just before running off towards the bathroom. "Did I mention you're the best?!" he said. "Be right back, I need to tinkle my wrinkle!"

"Yeah, you need to come up with a new phrase for going pee is what you need to do."

"Tinkle tinkle tinkle!" He yelled while in the bathroom.

"Whatever boy! You just make sure you wash and sanitize those hands after tinkling your **wrinkle**."

Thomas washed up and came out, kissed Juliandra on the cheek and in a quick fashion wiped his hands on her shirt just before rushing to his chair.

"Oops! Sorry, I got some all over my hands," he said laughing.

"Thomas! That had better be water; tell me that is water."

"I told you, I missed and I had to like, use my hand to deflect the stream. I didn't want to dirty the new hand towels and I figured you're gonna wash that shirt anyway. So what the heck, right?"

"I swear Thomas, if this isn't water, I will impose domestic violence on you."

Thomas, still laughing, walked over to the refrigerator and grabbed a bottle of cold water then sat back down at the table across from Juliandra.

"Yes," he said smiling, "of course it's water. I would never do that to you. I love you way too much to wipe pee on you. I mean, that would just be crazy. Okay, so there may have been a little pee in there. I'm not sure. I think I washed it all off."

Juliandra sprang from her seat sparking Thomas to do the same. She chased him around the living room as he laughed and yelled out "I'm sorry. I'm sorry." It wasn't long before Thomas leaped onto the couch, grabbed a pillow, and held it over his head as if to hide.

"Help me Lord!" he screamed out. "Save me from this woman who would beat me for no apparent reason. Help me now! I'm innocent!"

Juliandra plopped herself right on top of him and began to pinch his body in multiple places causing him to twist and jerk around.

"Stop it, stop it! Okay, okay! There was no pee, no peeeee!"

"I know," she said. "I just wanted to pinch you because you're so cute."

By this time, rain had begun to pour from the sky, slamming down onto the ground and roof. Juliandra pulled the pillow from Thomas's hands revealing his smiling face.

"You now owe me a kiss in the rain," she said.

"Ummm, you know I hate going out in the rain."

"You owe me, let's go."

He knew she loved the rain and the romantic feeling that came from standing in it. He also knew that as much as he disliked getting wet fully clothed, nothing was going to stop him from kissing her.

"I'll be outside" she said, "waiting for you to kiss me."

Thomas grabbed his shoes, headed to the back door and opened it without walking through. His eyes were drawn to a beautiful silhouette only feet away. Juliandra was standing with her face pointed upward and arms crossed just feeling the raindrops. Thomas walked over and stood right in front of her, staring at the water as it landed then ran off her body.

He thought, *how lucky am I, not to be a poor raindrop only able to touch for a brief time.* Juliandra opened her eyes and reached for him. She wanted what she was owed.

Thomas moved closer, slowly caressed her cheek then gently placed his lips against hers. For him, it was nothing less than extraordinary each and every time, and of all the things he loved doing; kissing Juliandra was by far his favorite. Life was spectacular in that moment, the sensation, captivating, and everything was perfect, until unexpectedly she pushed away.

"Doesn't count," she said.

"What? I thought that was good. I know how to kiss, and that was good."

"It was good, but it didn't count because you have to be barefoot in the rain to make it count."

"I have no idea where that rule came from, but I guess rules are rules."

Thomas removed his shoes, tossed them over his shoulders, and without pause reasserted his embrace. As the rain continued to pour, the two swayed, side to side, in the motion of a slow dance. It was more than a moment for him; it was hers' as well. He could tell and knew it to be true. Their steps went uninterrupted except for one brief instant when Juliandra looked into his eyes, smiled, and thanked him for coming outside.

"You don't have to thank me," Thomas said, "I'd go anywhere with you. You… are my soul mate, and I am bound to you. Where you go, I go."

"Awww, Thomas, I love you so much. Does that include my mom's house, on Friday?"

"Ooh, well, I really meant that figuratively, but why would we be going?"

"My mom wants to go to the cemetery and visit my dad's grave for a little bit, and she always feels better when Brighten and I are with her."

"Brighten's going? GOD, your brother doesn't stop bashing me whenever he's around. Can I just be there in spirit?"

Juliandra looked at Thomas and did her best to create a sad face.

"Okay, okay," he said. "I'll go because I love you that much, and besides without you, my Chinese food wouldn't taste so good."

"What? What do I have to do with your Chinese food? Ohh, you mean because I bought it and just handed it to you, so it tastes that much better."

"No, although, that is a very good point, and I will calculate that into my likes and dislikes from now on. What I mean is that everything in the world is better now that you're in my life. I can't explain it other than, well... music has more depth, the sun just feels nicer when it shines on me, the days mean more, and food, like my sesame chicken, just taste better. I don't know why, I just know that's how it is."

Juliandra reached out and hugged him firmly. "Thank you Thomas," she said. "I'm lucky to be with you, and I love you very, very much." She leaned back a little and smiled. "By the way I think one of your shoes went onto the roof."

"Really? I guess you owe me now, huh?"

Thomas began to sway again, leading her in another slow dance while the rain poured down. They stayed there, outside, moving back and forth for several minutes until Thomas stopped, picked her up and held her in his arms while she giggled.

"Time to pay up!" he said.

Thomas brought Juliandra inside, kicked the backdoor shut, and carried her into the bathroom. He started the shower and began to slowly remove her clothes...

CHAPTER 11 - THE MEETING

A burning sense of urgency drags Thomas off memory lane and back to reality where all focus shifts solely to the current predicament. Right now, he's got the upper hand and must use it in the extreme if he's to make this work. His feet had already stepped over the line and carried him across the moral boundaries which use to seem so far away. The next steps didn't seem like a huge stretch anymore; besides, there was no turning back, forward is the only direction.

Next, he must drive almost six hours to Houlton, Maine near the Canadian border to meet with another dangerous killer while under the guise of a contractor named Brian Johnson. They are to meet at the Community Park to discuss a fictitious job Jason told Roy he was being hired for, and Thomas needed extra time to scout the area before-hand to come up with a way to restrain and question him without being seen. Satisfied he's obtained enough information from Jason and Chief, Thomas heads back to the room and gathers everything needed for the trip. He collects all the papers, their wallets, car keys and cell phones, puts it all in one of Jason's travel bags and heads down to the rented minivan parked outside.

The address for the park is entered into the GPS and Thomas sighs as the estimated time, five hours forty minutes pops up. He reaches into a bag, pulls out an energy drink and chugs it down. Driving long distances was on his top ten list of hated things, and all the driving he was about to do wasn't going to be easy without the ability to sleep. A quick toss of the empty bottle into the back seat and his foot presses down on the gas pedal.

Five hours in and Thomas continues to repeat, out loud, every detail possible, phone numbers, locations, items, placements, distances, it all mattered. He needed to know everything by heart, plus the sound of his own voice seemed to help a bit to ward of the sandman. *Just keep focused,* he thinks. *Focus on the task at hand.*

Eventually, the repetition comes at a price; it starts to numb his mind and he needs to shake it off. Loud music worked in the past so the radio is turned up and tuned to a local station playing rock ballads. It was strange, some people got energy from heavy metal or hard rock, but Thomas always drew it from more subtle genres. He could work out or train while listening to slow songs rather than so called high-energy mixes. Unfortunately, everything he hears seems to have little meaning and does nothing except fill the van with noise, meaningless annoying noise. It was worse than the numbness. In one fell swoop the radio was silenced and his voice raised. The annoyance of the music worked though. It gave his mind a break; it was just what he needed to get back to the details.

The sun is starting to rise and Thomas has just arrived in the park with a few spare hours to walk the grounds and come up with a plan. He parks by a building opposite a large baseball field containing soccer goals towards the back. This is where Roy said to meet and Thomas intended on making sure he could find a private spot to question him when the time came. The building was locked, but he was able to force open the rusted metal door with a little help from the front bumper of his rental vehicle. After gaining entry, Thomas swings the door almost shut and parks the van in front of it to hide the damage. Everything looked good from outside, so he goes inside to investigate.

It was a graveyard of equipment, at least that's what it looked like. Ripped mats, sun bleached signs, crushed cones, PVC pipe everywhere, and some old mesh netting from a broken soccer goal which he grabs and sets by the door. There was a lot more old equipment piled up in different sections, but nothing really caught his eye until stumbling upon a rack full of baseball bats.

"Yes!" he says out loud, "now that's what I'm talking about."

Thomas starts picking them up one by one checking the feel and swinging each back and forth. Sadly, the idea of choosing a baseball bat for its 'knock someone in the head' properties would have been pretty odd just hours ago, but at the moment was all too normal. The fifth one felt pretty good, it was small and made of metal, lighter than the rest, and it would be easy to grab and quicker to swing. It's put in the minivan on the floor in front of the passenger seat then a larger wooden one placed near the entryway of the building. For the next few minutes Thomas practices different ways of walking through the entrance and using the second bat as a weapon to disable someone walking behind him. Over and over he steps outside then walks back in, grabbing it with his left hand and swinging it right at head level.

Soon he had it down and moved on, making another round through the building seeking out useful items. While walking Thomas pauses for a second, realizes just how tired he's become and heads to the van to get another energy drink. Remaining alert was imperative. He couldn't slip up or he'd risk having to start all over. So far, fighting off the drowsiness wasn't too difficult by keeping busy, but it was becoming harder and harder to do. It was a good time to walk the grounds outside, just to keep moving, while waiting for the ingredients to take effect. Thomas heads over on foot to the baseball field directly

134

across from the parking lot and looks inside the team dugouts, making sure to keep an eye on the building and van the whole time. The structures were unimpressive, overly simple, and seemed lifeless without the players stuffed in them. They were open and highly visible which would not work well for questioning someone, though he could envision each as good lookout spot to keep an eye on the roads coming into the park.

This hypothesis is proven true when he spots a silver sport utility vehicle entering and approaching the equipment building he's been rummaging through. Immediately, his heart starts beating faster, his hands begin to shake a bit, and his nervous system jumps to high alert. He feels caught off guard and underprepared, but makes his way to the vehicle which has now stopped behind his van, almost as if to block it in. Without hesitation, he walks to the driver's side window and sees a middle aged male with glasses holding a map of the area. Thomas knocks, distracting him from the map and queuing him to roll the window down.

"Roy?" Thomas asks.

"Uh, no," says the man. "My name is Pete." "My son has a game out here today and we're looking for the spot where we have to meet with his team."

Thomas looks in, behind the driver, and sees a young boy wearing a soccer jersey, tapping away on a cell phone. "I thought there were no games today," he says. "At least there aren't supposed to be any."

"Well, there's a soccer game here at noon and we're just a little early. I thought your car belonged to one of the parents, so I pulled in. People should be arriving in droves pretty soon."

"Are you sure your game's not on the bigger soccer field past those tennis courts?"

Thomas takes a step back from the window to point, and when he does several vehicles come into view, all turning toward the other field. Among the herd of new arrivals is a blue mid-sized car which has detoured left and pulled in behind the sport utility vehicle. It had Canadian plates and two men seated in the front. *Don't panic,* Thomas thinks, *they're probably coaches from Canada here for the game.*

The driver looks for a few seconds then begins to back up and turn the car around. Thomas quickly runs over waving his arms back and forth to stop them from leaving.

"Wait! Wait! Stop!" he yells out.

The vehicle stops and the driver rolls down the window. Thomas leans down a bit and sees the two men are dressed in jeans and t-shirts. *Huh,* he thinks. *They could be here for the game.* "Are you looking for the game or are you here to see Coach Johnson?"

"Coach Johnson," the driver replies.

Thomas leans closer to the window "Let me get rid of this soccer dad," he says. "He's confused about where the game is."

The driver gets out of his car and walks with Thomas, takes a quick look inside the silver vehicles windows and starts speaking to the man with glasses.

"Sir, the game is over there. You need to drive that way past the first field."

The lost soccer dad puts his map down and looks, confirming cars are indeed driving that way. "You guys are right," he says. "I better get over there before my son has to sit out for being late."

"Alright, have a good game," Thomas says. "You can just drive around this building and exit on the other side."

While the SUV slowly pulls forward and drives off, Thomas nervously tries to figure out a new plan to deal with the addition of a second person. It wasn't something he'd foreseen and definitely a terrible surprise.

Once out of view, the driver of the blue car walks back to his vehicle, gets in, and moves it beside Thomas's van. Both men climb out and the driver walks around the outside of the building as the passenger watches Thomas and looks through the windows of his minivan.

Thomas looks right at the passenger and asks. "Are you Roy?"

"Are you Brian Johnson?" He replies

"Yes, I am."

"Jason made it sound urgent that we meet with you Mr. Johnson. **What** is so urgent?"

"I was told I was meeting someone named Roy here."

"I'm Roy and so is he," the man says. "What are we doing here?"

"You mean you and him are both Roy? You're both named Roy?"

"Mr. Johnson, Brian, whatever the hell your name is, when someone begins to ask too many questions the mood changes, and I'm not sure I am in the mood for too many questions. Now, if you don't tell me why we're here, Roy is going to leave and before Roy leaves, you will cease to be."

"Sorry, I'm confused, but I need Roy to take someone out. My boss, he's screwing my wife and has treated me like shit for five years."

"Take someone out? Take out your boss? Where will we take him Mr. Johnson, on a date?"

The two men laugh for a few seconds before the driver walks up to Thomas and begins to push him towards the back of the building.

"What the hell guys?" Thomas complains. "No need to push. If you want to talk elsewhere we can all just walk nicely."

The driver punches Thomas in the back causing him to wince and stumble a bit. "We're not here to walk nicely, so shut up and keep quiet," he says. "Now, raise your arms above your head."

Both men search through Thomas's pockets and thoroughly pat him down before shoving him against the wall of the building.

"Are you a cop?" The driver asks.

"No, I'm a pissed off husband and I want the guy fucking my wife dead," Thomas says.

"Did Jason tell you the cost?"

"No, I hadn't really thought about the cost. I just want it done, and I'm willing to give you guys what I have."

"Well, Mr. Johnson, Roy is not cheap."

"I figured that. I'll pay the price whatever it is. I just want the guy gone."

"So, Jason didn't say anything about the cost to you?"

"I didn't ask. I just assumed it would be expensive."

The passenger of the car steps forward. "I have an issue with that," he says.

"What issue?" Thomas replies.

"Nobody meets without knowing the cost."

"I told you, I didn't ask him. I just told him I wanted to meet. I didn't ask!"

The Driver pulls out a pistol and points it at Thomas, nods to the passenger, and tells him to check around front.

"You know what I think?" The driver says. "I think you're full of shit and you're going to die today, right here."

A loud whistle is heard causing the driver to push Thomas against the building again. He steps close and then peaks around the side. It was another lost family roaming around looking for the game. While he watches his partner deal with the stray car, Thomas watches him and the gun pointed in his face. Thomas is extremely fearful and worried his chance to find out more is going to be over. Suddenly, he realizes the guy is preoccupied with what his partner is doing and wasn't really paying attention to him. *Now, now! It's got to be now*, he thinks. Thomas starts to slowly raise his left hand and shift his body weight onto the right leg. Then, in a quick motion, Thomas moves left grabbing the man's wrist behind the gun to complete a wristlock he'd done hundreds of times in class. He grabs tight, tighter than ever before, and bends the man's wrist downward, forcing him to drop to the ground.

"Go ahead; pull the trigger if you want." Thomas tells him.

The man looks at Thomas, clearly surprised. He'd been taken off guard by a nobody and almost seemed embarrassed about it. That notion and expression dissolve quickly after Thomas kicks his temple, knocking him unconscious. Thomas grabs the gun, runs to the opposite side of the building then watches the man's partner finish his interaction. When the lost family's car pulls away the second man starts walking toward the back, and Thomas moves in behind. Quietly, he maneuvers around the two vehicles, staying out of site until reaching the rear corner, at which time the pace is accelerated before jumping up and kicking the man's back. The move succeeds only in driving the guy forward and not to the ground, forcing Thomas to sprint again, tackling him instead. The struggle for dominance begins and the passenger proves challenging to control, so Thomas wraps his left arm around the man's neck, rolls to his back then uses a hip heist technique to stand and deliver knee strikes. The fourth blow ends the struggle, leaving the second person, known as Roy, lying face down, motionless. Thomas tries to stand, but midway stops to lean and vomit. "Fuckin ay!" he says. "If I get through this, I'm learning more Jiu-Jitsu."

Knowing the only chance to get answers and prevent a future struggle was to disable both men, Thomas moves quickly to hyperextend each of their elbows and one knee. The sound and feel each joint made while tearing was horrible, making the urge to vomit again strong, but he holds it back and continues focusing on the task at hand. It was supposed to become easier, easier to cross the line, and easier to hurt someone. It wasn't, and his old moral compass still remained, limiting him along the journey.

The driver is first to regain consciousness and attempt to scream out, causing Thomas to grab the wooden bat by the door and stand over him prepared to swing.

"I'd stay quiet if I were you. Too many screams changes the mood and I'm not in the mood for screams."

The injured killer quiets, but continues to move, groaning and trying to talk.

"Now, I have some questions for you two, and I'm really running out of patients. I'm just so sick of bad guys, and I am really, really tired. Here's how this is gonna work. I'm going to ask a question and if you don't give me the answer I need, a bone is going to break. Please, just answer the questions, there's been enough pain and suffering, I only want answers." Thomas leans over the man and loosens the netting which holds the rags in his mouth. "If you scream out I **will** use this on you, do you understand?"

"Yes. What do you want? What have you done to me?"

"I want to know who Roy is."

"We are Roy. We work as a team named Roy."

"You're both in a team… and it's called Roy? What the hell is Roy? Who names a team Roy? Are there more of you?"

"Yes, in fact, more of us are going to be here any minute. You should let us go right now."

Thomas shakes his head and walks over to the driver's right leg.

"I really hate this part," he says. "I only want answers. That's all I ever want from you guys." He raises the bat high in the air with both hands ready to swing downward.

"Okay, okay! It's just us, only the two of us. It's just us two. Don't, please!"

"Were both of you working yesterday morning? Were you and your partner, Roy number two, on Rosewater Avenue to shoot a girl named Juliandra?"

"No, I don't know any Juliandra?"

Thomas swings the bat down, striking the driver in the shin with enough force to crack the bone, then shoves the handle into his mouth to silence the pain filled screams.

"I'm going to ask you again," he says. "Were both of you on Rosewater Avenue yesterday morning to kill a girl named Juliandra?"

As Thomas eases the pressure, slowly pulling the bat away to let the driver speak, sounds of groaning start to pour from the second man who's begun to wake.

"Looks like I have two candidates for questioning now Roy number one."

"Please," the driver says. "I'll answer your questions. I will answer them."

Thomas looks back and forth comparing each of their faces.

"Ohh," he says, "don't tell me this guy's your brother or something. Wait... he is, isn't he? You two started a family business of killing people? Oh my God man, what the hell? Listen, all I want are some answers and then I'm gone. Did you kill a girl named Juliandra yesterday morning?"

"Yes, yes, a girl in a police car. Yes, her name was Juliandra."

"That was my wife you fuck! You killed my wife!"

"What do you want? Tell me what do you want?"

"I want to know exactly where you were between 8:36am and 9:36am. I wanna know where you were hiding, what position you were in, and I want to know every fart that came out of your ass! Where were the two of you?"

"He was at a house on Title Road, the people left for the weekend. It was... it was uh... 1628 Title Road. I was a mile east waiting for the call to come get him."

"How far from my house was he? How far from Juliandra?"

"About 320 yards north."

"What were you driving?"

"I drove a green Ford Taurus."

"Did you each have a prepaid phone?"

"Yeah, yeah, we always use a prepaid phone."

"I need both numbers. If you don't have those numbers start preying now to whatever deity you believe in. And, tell me exactly how you two worked this job together."

Thomas pulls out a pad, the same he used in Boston to note every important detail he got from Jason and Chief. The list was about to grow, so he flips to a blank page and listens as the injured driver talks. There was no way to verify what this person, this killer was telling him, but at least he was getting something, some idea to go by, and it was better than nothing.

"Now," Thomas says, "I need to know exactly where your partner was in the house. Which way he was facing, what he had with him, and what doors were unlocked. That means I have to question him because you weren't there. I don't have any desire to hurt him more, but if he doesn't answer my questions this bat is going to see some strikes."

Thomas shoves the rag back in the driver's mouth, tightens the netting holding, then walks over to the second man lying on the floor to begin the process all over again. You could just hear the yells and screams of soccer fans from outside as the players moved up and down the field over two hundred yards away. An hour and a half goes by before Thomas walks out of the building into the parking lot. He stands almost motionless, listening to the sound produced by the huge crowd of strangers gathered in one spot, each with a different life story, a different history to remember, and a different vision of the future. Every single one could have their life altered in the blink of an eye. How oblivious they all were to what was going on in the world. And then he thought. *Good for them.*

It was time to go... and meet with Boon.

CHAPTER 12 – THE HUNT

The sun is bright, the sky blue, and the scenery undoubtedly beautiful through the eyes of someone else. At the moment, the light beaming in through the windshield is nothing more than a reason for Thomas to push his sunglasses, just a bit closer to his face. He's on a nine-hour trek to the most famous city in the world with a foggy mind and clear mission. The drive is absolute torture, and besides consuming heavily caffeinated liquids, stopping every hour seems to be the only way to prevent dozing. Three times he has pulled over to walk around, stretch, and shake it off. Now, only five more stops remain before arriving in New York City. The whole time, Thomas continually recites, out loud, all the phone numbers, locations, and positions written down, until eventually no longer needing to look at the written words.

His strategy was simple at first, just get to them one by one and start hitting really hard. But, each new piece of information causes the plan to evolve. Ideas are spinning, swirling in a whirlwind of choices constantly growing, and with every spare neuron he shuffles through the options. *I could call each of them and plead for her life. No, that's ridiculous. I could call Jason Brean to plead for her life or offer more money to call it off. No, that will never work. I could call the police and tell them exactly where each of the shooters are going to be. No, they wouldn't believe me. These guys don't care and won't stop because they have a contract. The wheels are already in motion, and when something's in motion you need to ram it with something else in motion. Staying still isn't an option.*

No matter how much he knew, Thomas couldn't think of a way to prevent Juliandra's death without neutralizing each of the killers one at a time. *So be it,* he thinks, *it is what it is, and right now, my mission is to find out where Boon **was,** then stop him.*

The road starts to blur and sound begins to fade as Thomas's eyelids get heavier and heavier. It was time for another break. He slows the van and comes to a gradual stop on the side of the road, giving him a place to get out and walk to ward off the desire for sleep. After a few paces it was apparent walking alone wouldn't cut it, so he drops to the ground and starts counting pushups until his arms begin to give out. Thomas almost reaches fifty before jumping to his feet and sprinting back and forth to increase his heart rate. It was a terrible feeling being extremely wired and sleepy at the same time. A couple more sprints and another sensation hits him, hunger. The act of eating hadn't crossed his mind since waking up, and his body was demanding action. Into the van and onto the road once again, this time, to find food.

Exit by exit, Thomas reads the signs, seeking out a decent place to buy a meal. Every name was familiar, but not one felt right. In fact, nothing at all seemed appealing. Even his favorite places had little meaning and couldn't capture his attention as they did only days ago. He decided it didn't really matter, and the very next restaurant, diner, or fast food joint would be the one. It wasn't long before another exit sign came into view accompanied by a list of amenities. *Great!* He thinks, *food, hotel, and gas on the next exit.* Thomas veers right and heads down the curved pavement leaving the interstate. As the off ramp ends his heart speeds up and eyes open a little wider when the diner he and Juliandra ate in, that first evening, pops into sight.

"Figures!" He yells. "Awesome! More ways to torture my ass in this hell. Just shove it right up my ass!"

Plenty of parking spots remain and Thomas wastes no time navigating between two weathered lines to occupy one. Getting out of the van was quick and efficient. Going inside however turned out to be another story. He meant to walk right in, but for several minutes Thomas stands, motionless, looking at the sign mounted to the front. He had no words or thoughts, only emotions associated with the moments spent inside. His initial response was wrong. It wasn't the universe laughing about it, mocking him, or trying to increase the pain of his loss. It was a virtual pat on the back, a thumbs up to right the wrong, and a nod of understanding to acknowledge it. If anything, being there reinforces his will to go on.

He steps through front entrance and is seated in a booth behind a family with children, one baby and two older, maybe three to four years of age. The older kids seem to think his presence is better than being at a theme park, or eating, since clearly that was no longer their interest. Exempt from any care of the world, they continually turn and stare, displaying a barrage of honest expressions. It was a welcome distraction, but only for a few seconds. Thomas didn't have the luxury of feeling amused or entertained; he had plans to go over and other thoughts to contend with. Focus had to shift to the pad lying on the table, so his eyes move away, downward to review it.

"Hi," a small voice calls out.

Thomas looks up to see the little girl in the next booth waving. He smiles back and she quickly turns away and slowly looks back again.

"You look sad," she says.

The child's mother immediately reprimands her. "Julie, leave that man in peace. Now turn around and stop bugging people."

147

Thomas politely smiles. "It's no problem," he says.

"But, he's sad," the girl explains to her mother.

"Okay, leave him alone and face this way."

Thomas looks down again at his notes and continues to ponder the logistics and tactics required to save Juliandra. Soon, a body stops near him causing his eyes to turn and readjust. It was a waitress. Her badge was pinned on crooked and had a white label stuck to it, spelling out her name in small black letters. She exuded patients, and seemed calm considering no one else was waiting tables.

"Hi, my name is Elodie. Can I get you a drink while you look over the menu, or do you already know what you want?"

Thomas picked up the menu, pointed to one of the dinner specials and asked for water along with it.

"Would you like to change any of the sides that come with it?" She asked.

"No," he replied. "I'll take everything as it shows on the menu."

"Well, that makes my life easy. I'll be right back with your drink, and your order should be out fairly quick."

"Thank You." Thomas says.

Elodie walks away, and within seconds is back with and empty glass and pitcher of cold water. She fills the glass and heads to another table recently abandoned by an older couple taking tiny steps towards the door. Thomas watched as the waitressed bounced, like a pinball, around the dining area taking care of people and cleaning up after them. She was a den mother for all

148

who came in, unappreciated and taken for granted by most. *That woman is someone's daughter*, he thinks. *Maybe someone's wife or sister, a human being not a robot dispensing treats. Man people piss me off.*

The next stop brings Elodie back to Thomas's table where she drops off his meal and bounces to the next location. It doesn't take long to shovel the majority of it down. Taste wasn't important. Neither was texture. It was fuel and that was all. He was almost done when the family with kids got up to leave. They looked like a group of ducks getting ready to make their way to the next swimming hole, parents in front and kids in tow. Just as they begin to move the little girl falls out of line and stops in front of Thomas to wave. The mother's head shakes slightly, left and right before handing a baby carrier to her husband.

"Leave that man alone Julie." she says. "Let him finish his meal, we're leaving."

Thomas looks at the miniature person standing only inches away and who has no intention of being diverted from her mission to cheer him up.

"Julie is a very pretty name," he says. "My wife's name was Juliandra."

"Joolandra is pretty too." She replies. "Where is your wife?"

The mother calls out again and heads toward the booth. "I said, leave that man alone Julie. Now, get your bag, and let's move it." The woman looks at Thomas. "I'm sorry mister; she'll talk your ear off if you let her."

"It's okay," Thomas says. He looks down at the walking smile named Julie. "My wife is gone now." He tells her.

The little girl doesn't hesitate, nor does she ask permission, she simply steps closer and gives Thomas's left arm a hug. "She will come back," she says, "and you won't be sad anymore."

Another smile and she releases his arm then runs to get her small red bag.

"O geez, sorry again mister. I'm so sorry; she doesn't understand things like that yet. Come on Julie, let's go."

The little girl waves as they walk by and leave the building. *Unbelievable,* he thinks. *I'm in the middle of nowhere at some random all night diner, and some stranger's three year old daughter gives me the best motivating pep talk ever.*

The kid was honest, saw things as they were, and expressed herself without reservation or apology. There was no filter, and what she said was exactly what he needed to hear. Thomas gathered his notes, put everything into his pocket then flagged down the waitress to square up. Elodie walks over, but doesn't carry with her the usually miniature sized invoice associated with eating out. There was no paper in her hand or plastic check holder; instead, she brings an explanation of why there's no bill.

"The family that just left took care of it," she says. "They felt bad about their daughter hassling you, so they paid your bill."

"Really?" he says. "Wow, that never happens does it?"

"Not very often, but they were nice people."

"Well, I don't know what to say other than thank you."

"You're welcome. Stay as long as you like. No hurry."

He looked out the window and watched the family drive away, knowing everything was worth it.

There were good people in the world, mixed among the bad. And good people deserve a chance. Juliandra was a good person, the best in fact, and she deserved her chance, an opportunity to live and share her life with others. It's not about me. It's not about what I want. I've got to get her that chance, a chance to exist, and to be alive.

His sadness was now masked by another emotion. It wasn't anger, or rage. This time he felt, possibility. This time he felt hope. Hope for Juliandra and everything yet to come. Everything she meant and could mean again, what she stood for and would stand for in the future, all that she had given and all she could give before leaving the world. Thomas wanted her to live and continue shining no matter what his cost. And, if there had been any doubts before now, they were eradicated along with any deficiency of determination. It was time to un-pause and move on to New York.

Thomas hops in the rental, recharged, and with a new interpretation of life, his place within it, and the role that must be played. His mind is racing thinking of ways to get answers from the next stranger who's defined only by actions, a short description, and singular name. All he needed was a few details, enough to know where and how. The key's turned and the engine started. A quick look left, a swift glance right, a short gaze in the rear view mirror then straight ahead. This was going to be a one-way trip and he knew it. Once he got those answers he'd be facing the nightmare again.

The 10:00am meeting was in Time Square, so Thomas booked a room at a Hotel on the corner of West 42nd Street and 8th Ave. According to Jason, Boon would be standing by a hot dog vendor where 42nd and 9th intersect, and he'd wait exactly five minutes before leaving. Twice already, Thomas had been taken off guard and ended up barely surviving the confrontation. He couldn't risk that again. Not at this point. This time he was going to try something different. He was going to let Boon wait those five minutes. He'd watch from a distance then follow until he had an opportunity to restrain him.

Surprisingly, the next four hours go by with relative ease compared to the first, and Thomas arrives at the hotel without nodding off. It was a combination of loud music, cool air and pure determination preventing his body from claiming its next requirement. He pulls the van into the valet area, grabs what he needs then hands the vehicle off like a baton during a relay race. The thing had served its purpose and was no longer necessary, just like the discarded drink containers tossed aside after being emptied.

Off the pavement and through the glass doors he walks making his way to the lobby, clutching tightly to one bag in particular the entire time. From check-in to the elevator, down a hallway, and finally through the entry way of room 422, his grip doesn't loosen until the door closes behind him. Even then the release is made with hesitation. It was the bag from Boston containing all that was important, and all that was gained to this point. Though he had already spent much time continually reciting number after number, detail after detail, he still wanted to review everything, every bit of it, laid out and in plain view. The thought of having to repeat the process was motivation enough to ingrain the knowledge and never forget it.

He placed his hand drawn map on the bed then the cell phones, and finally all the notes he's become intimately familiar with throughout the journey. His eyes fixate on the map, the one thing he couldn't analyze while driving, and for the next few hours he scrutinizes, inspects, ponders and stares, looking at the angles, trying to determine the best routes to each location and thinking about what actions to take once there. Idea after idea was scrambled and mixed together. It was getting harder to think, at least clearly. It was also taking longer and longer to formulate, imagine, and reason the steps. Time felt as if it were moving slower than before, but that was not the case for his level of alertness which had been dropping drastically during the last half hour. It was quickly reaching a new low and Thomas needed another break, so he decides to go out and explore the streets in an effort to regain his wits. He needed stimulation, and that was something New York would absolutely never have a shortage of.

1:00am was only two minutes away but there were still nine hours between him and Boon. *What on earth am I going to do for nine hours?* He thought. The city definitely contained an abundance of activity and offered plenty to do round-the-clock, but he couldn't think what direction to go. The only lucid thing at the moment was the need to physically move and in the end it didn't really matter which way. Left, right, forward, backward, it was all motion. Notes in hand, Thomas takes a step and begins walking, wondering around Time Square going from place to place in disbelief. He never realized how many people were actively doing things throughout the night. Of course everyone knows this to be the case. To experience it though, that was different; that was another level of understanding.

Diners, pubs, bars, and anything in between open for business became a mental respite. It was hard however to throw time

153

away or waste it when the objective was to do so. Hours were passing, but not like he'd hoped. It felt more like watching a puddle of oil evaporate, and everywhere he went the clocks ran at the same pace, like cold honey poured from a pinhole. But, the scenery changed and the bustle surrounding him provided a bit of energy, enough to keep him going. Thomas was learning too, not about his goals or objectives, about people, and how they behave when crammed into small spaces. The city was big, but with all those human beings in one place it sure seemed small.

Walking amongst the population turned out to be an interesting experience, almost like studying changes in a social petri dish. One observation in particular, plain and prominent, no one was paying attention, not to him anyway. They didn't seem to notice his presence or acted as if he wasn't there. *You could become invisible*, he thought, *like a ghost until you stopped to buy something, and even then once the transaction was complete, you'd be a ghost again.*

Literally, tons of individuals moving all the time, in and out of buildings, up and down sidewalks, and every one of them ignoring bodies only inches from their own. If an assessment had to be made it would be that most trained themselves to see others more or less as moving obstacles. Something to avoid or navigate around, and they probably didn't view them as people anymore. There were too many, the brain can't process that many individuals. Perhaps certain ones could be seen as an opportunity, or a nuisance, but nothing more. And, if you spoke to someone, just to say hello, you might risk appearing abnormal, an oddity which didn't belong.

Despite the torturously sluggish pace at which time progressed, Thomas eventually emerged from an all-night diner into daylight. Nine hours had passed since he left the hotel and ventured into the streets. Was it reality or a dream? He couldn't tell anymore. His heart was racing, but his body wanted to collapse and shut down. It was demanding rest, the one thing that couldn't be given, not yet, not now. He walked to 42nd and 9th Ave and stood by an ATM to get a good view of the opposite corner. *So many people,* he thought, *it never stops with so many people roaming the streets day and night.* The good thing was anyone standing still looked out of place. If you weren't moving, you could easily be identified like a prey animal straying from the herd. Because of this Thomas did his best to appear occupied by writing notes, looking at papers, and pacing around as he watched for anyone not in motion, anyone who looked out of place.

Finally, 10:01 arrives and a person appearing stagnant falls into his vision. It was a man wearing cargo shorts carrying a camera and walking around very little. The guy was thin and had long hair which receded in front just as described by his associates. *This has to be him,* he thinks, *there's nothing on that intersection to take pictures of.* The man's movements quickly develop into a noticeable pattern, and it becomes evident the curious picture taking tourist look was a rouse. By 10:04 he had circled around and snapped shots of the same things three times.

As promised, when the time advanced to 10:05, the camera wielding individual immediately started walking down 9th Ave, away from the corner. Thomas wastes no time and crosses 42nd Street to follow, staying several yards behind. He keeps pace until 41st Street where the man veers off to the left and walks into a parking garage. At this point Thomas jogs to the entrance then carefully walks in, looking to see where the last killer went. His eyes dart back and forth trying to capture any glimpse of motion. Nothing left, nothing right. Faint sounds of cars running, rolling, and accelerating filled the structure, but one unique sound broke the ambient norm and stood out. It was a universal ding sound which echoed through the lower level. Thomas's eyes move at light speed to focus on the elevator. One by one his feet advance in that direction, increasing speed along the way. The next sound was that of the elevator doors opening which triggered another shift in pace. The killer has stepped in and was focused on the button panel. As the entrance gets closer Thomas pulls the van key from his pocket and places it between the index and middle finger to use as makeshift weapon. Just when the man's hand reaches to press a number, Thomas sprints in, collides at full speed, and drives him into the back wall of the small box.

Instantly, the struggle begins as Thomas blocks, ducks, bobs, and weaves to avoid getting hit by stray shots from his opponent's rapidly swinging arms. Everything's moving at lightning speed and the guy fighting back seems well versed in art of trading punches. Thomas stays close and grabs hold despite the impacts occurring to the top of his head and brow. Back and forth the two slam hitting each wall over and over as they battle to control an unpredictable outcome. The key, held between Thomas's fingers has fallen to the floor blending with a collage of camera parts scattered along its surface, and the fight, though only seconds old, was taking too long. It had to end before someone realized it was happening or came upon the scene. Either scenario would prevent questioning of the last murderer. A quick shove and Thomas moves back. As soon as enough space develops, he kicks the man's left knee then strikes his lip and nose with an elbow. The blows create an opportunity that's not wasted as he immediately grabs behind the man's neck and begins driving knees into his body. Finally, a second elbow strike to the jaw causes the individual to buckle and drop, scattering plastic parts in every direction.

Ding.

The elevator bell rings once more as if to signal the end of a round, and the metal doors start to open. Fearing the exposed entrance might reveal an innocent bystander on the other side, Thomas reaches down and pulls the man to his feet, thinking somehow it would minimize the appearance of conflict. At that moment, a loud arc sound fills the small space accompanied by sharp pain. The third killer was no novice and had come prepared. Thomas could do nothing but watch as the answers he sought staggered away. *Great!* He thinks. *All that and I get Zapped! This is why you break their damn arms and legs right away. I was doing so good with that.*

Within seconds, Thomas is able to move freely and doesn't let any time pass before putting that mobility to use. Two keys are visible on the floor near him, one his, and the other most likely from his opponent. Both are collected before standing up and peering out into the large area filled with cars. Nothing, no one was visible. No motion, no movement, no nothing. Thomas runs out and across the garage to the opposite end. *The man must be near his car,* he thinks. *He probably doesn't even know he dropped his key, so he must have run towards his car.*

He raises his hand and starts pressing the lock button on the key's integrated radio transmitter, triggering the momentary horn blast. Eventually, he's able to zero in on the cars location and starts carefully moving towards it. On the way, a silhouette whisks across his field of view. It was him, the third killer, a predictable human after all, just like the rest of us. Thomas gives chase and quickly catches up, cornering the man who's now wielding a mini stun gun in plain view. The high voltage which paralyzed him a moment ago was now being thrust in his direction from multiple angles. Thomas pulls the belt from his waist and wraps a good portion around each of his hands, leaving about one foot between them. Each time the man's wrist gets close Thomas tries to capture it with the unwrapped part. On the fifth attempt his timing works and the belt takes hold, allowing him to pull the man off balance and avoid getting shocked. Using all his body weight, Thomas yanks left and right until he's able to trip him.

Once down, he steps in and grabs the wrist, holding it in a locked position with the stun gun pointed away. Using the pain induced by hyperextending the joint he coerces the man into flipping on his stomach where he's able to bend the arm up and back, freeing the weapon.

"Boon!" Thomas says. "I have some questions for you."

A pain filled voice replies. "I'm not Boon, you got the wrong guy."

Thomas takes the belt and ties the man's wrists behind his back then begins searching pockets.

"Ahh, a cell phone. What's the swipe pattern Boon?"

"Screw you man. I know my rights. And, I told you I ain't Boon, whoever that is."

"Look, if you're not Boon, then I'll leave you alone, but to find out, I need to check your phone."

"Take me in cop and you can talk to my lawyer. That's all I'm sayin'."

"Oh, I'm no cop, just a concerned citizen. Now what's the swipe pattern of your phone?"

Thomas swipes a few times and then takes the Taser and places it on the man's neck. "Just give me the pattern, wait... just figured it out. Letter Z; how original."

A couple of taps and there it was in the call history, Jason Brean's phone number. Thomas was relieved and sick to his stomach at the same time. This was Boon, and he had to make him talk. Though angry, there was no enjoyment in hurting these guys. He kept telling himself it was just and for the right reasons, but it didn't feel that way. Thomas closes his eyes, takes in a deep breath then slowly exhales as he drops the phone into his back pocket. When his eyes open he flips Boon onto his back and delivers punch after punch until the voluntary movement of his body ceases.

Now, he's on the road once again, heading out of the city in Boon's vehicle. And, it wasn't long before the familiar sound of painful groaning began to emanate from the back seat. Boon had regained consciousness, and each time he attempted to scream out Thomas shocked him with the stun gun until he stopped. It seemed to be a good system and the cycle continued for roughly thirty minutes before a good place to pullover and question Boon was found. Once parked, Thomas turns to the back seat.

"Listen carefully," he says. "I need some answers to some very specific questions, and please just give me the answers. If you do, I'll call for help and walk away. If not, we've got a long day ahead of us."

"What have you done to me?" Boon asks.

Thomas lets out sigh and places the stun gun on Boon's face before turning it on.

"I ask the questions you fucking murderer! I broke your arms and legs, now answer my fuckin' questions or I'll shove this fucking thing in your eyes and keep it on until they burst!"

"Alright, alright," the man says. "What do you want to know?"

"Hmm, let's see. You and your pathetic piece of shit friends killed my wife Saturday. You shot her with a high-powered rifle. Where exactly were you at 8:36am that morning? And, I mean exactly where! Give me distance."

"I was in a barn, 1800 yards south west of your house waiting."

"But you moved didn't you? You shot Juliandra while she was in the police car out front, so you had to get closer."

Boon coughs a bit "Yeah, I moved. You guys were leaving, and my instructions were not to let that happen."

"And, if we hadn't tried to leave, you would've stayed in the Barn?"

"Yes, yes, the location was fine. There wasn't any other reason to move."

"What was the address?"

"I don't know the address. All I know is that it was on River Street and it was a big Barn with a silo next to it."

"Where exactly, were you in this barn? Tell me exactly where you were and which way you were facing."

"Jesus, man. I confessed what more do you want? You got me. You got me, now just turn me in."

Thomas takes the stun gun and places it near Boon's left eye

"I wonder just how long it would take?"

"I was up high, on a loft looking out a small opening in some doors."

"What did you bring with you? Tell me what you had in the Barn. I mean everything."

"I had two rifles, an M98B and an M40, a 45 pistol, a hunting knife, a rangefinder and prepaid cellphone. That's it."

"Now tell me where each of those things were and exactly where you placed them."

"I was holding the M98. The M40 was to my right. The rangefinder was on the left. My phone was on the floor below the M98 bipod. The knife and pistol were on me."

"Why two rifles?"

"It's just standard…"

"**Why!?**"

"The M40 was a backup in case I got closer."

"What if someone called you and said don't do it? Would you not take the shot?"

"No one ever does that. You don't cancel a job like that."

"What if they did, would you not do it?"

"Maybe, if the person who hired me called. But, they'd have to call, no one else."

There's no way Thomas would be able to speak with Jason that morning and convince him to call off all the killers, so the plan remains unchanged. He'll make his way on foot to 2499 Rosewater Ave and disable Chief, head to 1628 Title Road to stop the two men known as Roy, then use the Ford Taurus they drove to make it near the barn on River Street and prevent Boon from taking his shot.

The driver's side door opens and Thomas climbs out. He did it. He'd gotten what he came for. It seemed impossible but now felt easy compared to the challenge lying ahead. After a brief look around he starts walking, leaving the car behind with Boon inside. Step after step he moves down the street mumbling all the information he'd collected. Nothing else was on his mind, only the details, all those details. He had to remember, remember the addresses, phone numbers, where each person was at what time, and the positions of every item they had.

Several people standing on the sidewalk and passing on foot went out of their way to avoid him as he got near. He must have appeared crazy to them, a simple lunatic talking to himself. Their comments were easily heard, but Thomas didn't care about perception. It was about being in the moment and doing what he had to. The written notes from his pocket were now in his hand, ready for the next glance as he continued to speak aloud with only his own mind as the intended audience. The steady stride he kept was uninterrupted before coming upon a small group of teenagers walking the opposite direction. Each of the five youth were either laughing or pointing as someone yelled out the word loser, but Thomas was oblivious to it until one grabbed his notepad and ran off.

"Hey!" Thomas yells. "That's my paper! You stole my paper! Bring it back here!"

The kid continued to run, further and further away, as his friends carried on laughing and making comments. *"It didn't matter anyway"* Thomas thought, he got all he could in his head, and now it was time to leave, time to restart hell and fight. Eight more steps lead him to a utility pole which becomes a backrest after sitting. The sun warmed his face as he watched the cars drive by. The sound was soothing and the wind cool when it moved.

Slowly he closed his eyes and let go...

CHAPTER 13 - THE HOPE

A combination of warmth, comfort, and contentment is now the only thing surrounding Thomas. Slowly, his eyes open and that feeling rapidly changes to a sense of urgency as memories, assorted thoughts, and a mix of emotions surge in like ocean water slamming against a rocky shore. He turns... Juliandra is there, right beside him as if nothing ever happened. Automatically, without conscious thought his arms extend, reaching out to pull her close and hold tight.

"I love you, Juliandra," he whispers. "I love you more than anything."

A quiet sleepy voice replies. "I love you too, Thomas."

For him, holding Juliandra, if only for a few seconds, gave new meaning to the phrase 'live in the moment', and if that moment could last forever that's where he'd choose to be. But he couldn't. He had to go. He had to earn it.

Thomas grabs his phone, looks at the clock then eases out of bed. It was time to put all the information gathered thus far to work. The plan is to let Juliandra sleep while stopping each of the killers one at a time. It wasn't a perfect plan by any means, simple, straightforward maybe, but not perfect. It only needed to work. He had to make it work. Once in the living room, every detail was written out on paper. Phone numbers, addresses, items, and locations, nothing was left out. The paper went in his pocket along with some para-cord found in a kitchen drawer and a small pry bar from his toolbox. Chief will be first, and possibly a difficult first since he'd taken the precaution of locking the door behind him after breaking in to the house on Rosewater Ave. Fortunately for Thomas, Chief's method of gaining entry may have left the locking mechanism vulnerable.

It's 8:46am and every minute that could be spared has passed while preparing for the most important task of his life. It was now or never and Thomas had little use for hesitation, delay, or procrastination. Those words, their meanings, or any derivative of them were no longer part of his thoughts. Action was the only process, and now was the only time. Out the back door he heads, on foot, eastward through the trees. On paper, and in his mind, it seemed the most logical direction, but part way through it became clear the path was taking longer than expected to traverse. Thomas had to speed his pace which increased the risk of being seen or heard, a risk that had become necessary and vital to maintain the element of surprise. A risk which pays off after arriving, unnoticed, near the final destination. It was a section of the road across from and on the far side of the house where Chief said he was waiting.

The area was quiet and the need for stealth evident during his careful approach. A quick sprint to the south east corner and a quiet walk brings him to the front door which showed obvious signs of damaged. Thomas places his pry bar in what looks like the spot previously used to break in then slowly starts to apply force. The wood begins to compress and the metal parts scrape together, causing enough noise to make him stop and ease off. There needed to be a distraction, something to overshadow the sound. Thomas pulls out his cell phone and enters Chief's number, sets the pry bar back in place, and makes himself ready. A quick tap on the call button sets everything in motion. After the first ring the phone drops in a pocket, the pry bar is torqued, and the door rammed. Thomas runs full speed into the house, straight at first, then left into the bedroom harboring Chief.

Bewildered and taken off guard, the killer fumbles while reaching for his pistol, but it was too late. Thomas got to it first and was already on top of him, hammering the butt into the side of his head. The blows didn't stop until Chief's body became motionless. Thomas starts to tie him up with para-cord, but stops after remembering how Boon stunned him. He had to do it; he wasn't prepared to end a life, but he had to disable Chief to keep him from coming back into the fight. Within seconds both of Chief's elbows and one knee were hyper-extended, leaving him helpless and incapacitated. Sadly, Thomas's proficiency was increasing in this regard, and the more it did the more he hated it.

Chief's cell phone, rifle, and hand gun were collected then placed in an attic opening before checking the time. It was 9:08 and the plan was already failing. It took too long to get to and disable just one of the contracted killers. Two more remained and only one needed to pull the trigger. Out and into the back yard he runs, using the few trees around for cover on the way to Title Road. More precious seconds were being eaten up by stopping at each one momentarily before sprinting to the next, but eventually the east side of the home is reached. According to the Roy partners the front door had been left unlocked, one of them had not yet arrived, and the other, the triggerman, was in the middle of the kitchen aiming his barrel through a window. Thomas turns the doorknob slowly and pushes, just enough to look inside. He could see the shooter in a prone position on top of a table, preoccupied looking through a scope. It was a straight run with no obstacles and no reason to stop. A deep breath and Thomas drives forward with his shoulder, running full speed before leaping into the air and landing on the killer's back, instantly squeezing his neck with an arm choke. Everything, including the two men, slide and fall to the floor. The shooter struggles and tries relieving the pressure causing his senses to diminish, but nothing he does can loosen the hold.

Thomas won't let go until all movement stops and it's clear the shooter has lost consciousness. Within seconds he does, then, out of routine, Thomas lets out a sigh, grunts, and starts hyper-extending the man's joints.

9:18, and Roy number two remains one mile east, waiting in a car needed to reach Boon. Thomas picks up the shooter's phone, enters a number and taps the call button.

After the first ring, an answer. "Go," the voice says.

Sternly, Thomas replies. "It's done," and immediately disconnects.

Almost immediately the phone's display changes, showing an incoming call. It was the number he just dialed, but it goes unanswered.

9:19, Thomas searches the house, seeking anything to help disable the second member of Roy, but nothing seems right. Eventually, he grabs the rifle from the kitchen, walks to the front entrance and stands against the wall, waiting.

9:22, the brief quiet gets masked by sound from a car engine getting closer, triggering his grip to tighten and stance to ready. A dense wave of cool air suddenly slams his face when the door flies open and a man rushes in. Every muscle collaborates, tenses, and contracts to swing the rifle butt towards the figure calling out a name. A loud thud and the man's fate is sealed.

It was disturbing, Thomas thought, how easily a person could be broken. He never dwelled on it much before, but it almost sickened him to realize the fragility of a human being. All those times in school he'd been intimidated by some bully, or backed down from confrontation. Those fears were unwarranted; those kids were just as fragile as he was.

9:26, Thomas speeds down Rosewater Avenue towards River Street located just past his house on the left, but as the vehicle accelerates he notices someone standing outside. Instantly, their eyes lock and his foot switches pedals, engaging the brakes and causing the car to slide to a stop. Thomas calls out and pulls the door handle in an effort to exit, only to watch as Juliandra drops to the pavement. It was too late. Boon had shifted position and taken the shot early. The metal, glass, and plastic materials separating them feels like a brick wall ten feet thick as Thomas drives his body against the car door trying to move in her direction. It won't get out of the way fast enough, but when the gap is finally sufficient, he rushes over and drops to his knees, tears flowing uncontrollably. There was nothing he could do except cry when every emotion possible burst in all at once. So close, but he wasn't able to save her, this wonderful human being whose horrible fate was set years ago. She was gone.

Thomas doesn't move until the police arrive and force him to release his embrace of Juliandra. Shortly after, he finds himself being questioned yet again by Detective Davis in a small room. This time, however, there are no responses, no interactions of any kind. He chooses to remain silent and nothing they say can break that silence, and nothing they do can shift his focus. All outwards senses fade as his mind races, working at top speed, reviewing every mistake, choice, option, and possibility while stepping through hundreds of scenarios. Anything out of the ordinary will cause one of the shooters to pull the trigger early, and he'll need to work faster, get more efficient, and potentially do something he's never done before, take a life.

Frustration soon overcomes Detective Davis during his questioning, leaving him little choice but to hold Thomas as a suspect. Eventually, the night comes and Thomas closes his eyes with the hope he'll succeed next time they open. Four more times he finds himself sitting in that exact cell waiting for another chance to save Juliandra, but each attempt fails with the same result, Thomas holding her lifeless body and Boon getting away.

Confidence dwindles to an all-time low and self-doubt sweeps in like a hurricane; something must change. Morals are becoming an unacceptable obstacle. The concept is blurring like a faded memory, and the idea of killing each of them isn't looking so bad anymore. But, even if Thomas wanted, he couldn't use one of the other assassin's rifles to shoot Boon. They didn't have the range, only Boon's did. Thomas would have to get close before shooting and by that time, Juliandra would be dead. *There has to be a way,* he thinks. *It can't go on forever like this, it just can't.*

Night approaches once more as Thomas reviews the conversations with each killer during his interrogations of them. Everything is clear and nothing seems to stand out until something Brighten said pops into his mind. It was when they did research on Reggie and Professor Ledger. Brighten was upset because all he had to do was type his father's name into a search box and the answer he sought came right up. All his life he didn't know anything about Reggie's painful past, though it was already there just waiting for him to discover. Thomas knew what to do this time. His answer was already there. He just couldn't see it, but now he could, a possible solution that was in front of him the whole time.

Sure of himself and his new idea, Thomas closes his eyes and allows the darkness to take over yet again. Just as quickly as his mind drifts away a familiar warm feeling encompasses his body, triggering him to open his eyes, spring out of bed, and run into the living room. He grabs his work laptop and powers it on, brings up a search engine then begins to look for something called SMS spoofing. He'd run across this a few times while working in the field and it was the solution desperately needed. All the information he could find leads him to believe that it would be possible to send an anonymous message to each killer's cell phone in the guise of another person's number or name. Thomas grabs his wallet and creates an account on the site most talked about in forums he's quickly looked over then proceeds to formulate a message.

As a test, he uses the site to send himself an anonymous text using Jason Brean's cell number for the sender id. It took almost two minutes from the time he clicked send on the website for the message to show on his phone, but it looked legitimate, enough that it may pass for an actual message from Jason. It was go time and now or never for the new plan. A carefully thought out message was sent through the website to all four prepaid cell numbers used by the assassins, each identical, word for word.

SMS *"Eliminate the other two contracts now and your payment will triple."*

Thomas realized that he had been working too hard at directly stopping the killers when he could have had them working to stop each other. It was a revelation that he had not thought of before and now he needed to wait and see if the men believed it. After two minutes he runs to a front window, peaks out and mumbles.

"My money's on Boon you sons of bitches."

A shot is finally heard but it was from Chief's location not Boon's. *I was wrong*, Thomas thinks, *Chief was the go-getter first*. Another cracking sound echoes outside, this one was different, more distant than the first. Thomas knew it was Boon. Boon wasn't dumb; he let the other two battle first and then shot the winner. It seems both Chief and the first Roy are out of the picture, and now there was just Boon and the second Roy partner to deal with. Thomas is sure Boon will wait for the second Roy to show first and will shoot him, so he heads out the back door and runs to the house Chief occupied. After kicking in the door Thomas runs into the room where Chief lay dead, and without hesitation, reaches into the man's pocket for his car keys. Thomas knew exactly where they were and wasted no time heading directly into the garage towards the car Chief had parked inside.

Thomas hops in and turns the key. When the engine starts he slams the shifter into drive, stomps the gas pedal and speeds forward, smashing the vehicle through the unopen garage door. Thomas finds himself driving right behind the green Ford Taurus, driven by the second Roy who must have come from seeing his partner dead. The Ford suddenly decelerates, causing Thomas to collide with it's rear bumper, and the two vehicles come to a stop just past his own home where Juliandra stands, watching with a fearful expression. She screams when the driver of the green car climbs out and walks toward Thomas with a pistol in his hand. On the fifth step, just as he raises the gun to take aim, fragments of his skull and brain coat the surface of Chief's car.

"Boon!" Thomas yells out.

Thomas then quickly turns the steering wheel left, puts the vehicle in reverse, and backs up while lowering his head below the dash, until reaching Juliandra.

"Run in the house!" He yells. "Get in the house and lay on the floor! No time to explain."

Waving his hand, he repeats himself several times, but Juliandra refuses to move and insists on going with him.

"No Thomas!" Juliandra says. "I'm going with you. If you die I'll die anyway. I have to go with you!"

"You'll be killed Juliandra! If you go you'll die! I don't understand why you won't listen to me. There's no time for this, you've gotta go back in the house, now!"

"I won't stay while you go and get killed Thomas. I'm going with you. What happens happens. I have to go with you!"

Extremely confused, Thomas stares at her then looks straight ahead and finally back at Juliandra.

"Alright, stay right there, and don't move an inch! Okay?"

"Okay," she replies. "Yes, okay!"

Eyes forward and lost in thought, Thomas pauses before rapidly turning, grabbing two duffle bags from the back, and jamming one between the driver's seat and accelerator, causing the engine to rev up high. The second bag is propped up with Chief's baseball cap on top then the shifter pulled into drive, sending the car off towards the road.

Thomas grabs Juliandra's arm: "Let's go! We have to make it to that old barn down on River Street."

Three shots echo from the west along with the sound of glass shattering and falling to the ground. *He fell for it,* Thomas thinks. *Boon's probably moving towards the car right now to check on his handy work.* A few more steps and Thomas stops to pull Juliandra close.

"I want you to run." He says. "I want you to head east and keep going until you come out in the next neighborhood. You've got to go now while this man trying to kill you is distracted."

"No Thomas, I can't."

"You've got to, you have to go now, or you'll be shot! Do you understand that? I don't want you to die. I love you too much, so please... go."

"And what's that say about me, Thomas? That I was willing to run away while you got yourself killed. Never! I love you more than life itself, and if it's our time, it's our time together. No matter how..." Juliandra pauses, covers her eyes and looks away.

"No matter how? How what?" Thomas asks.

Juliandra wipes a tear from her eye and faces Thomas again. "I just love you so much."

"But this is your only chance Juliandra. Please... please go. I will never think any less of you, and I want you to live. You have to live. Please... for me."

"Thomas, look at me. I never told you this before because I didn't want to admit it. That first day we met, at the concert, when I saw your face and saw you smile at me. I knew. I knew I was going to love you. I knew at that moment you were my other half. Oh sure, I pretended it wasn't going to be easy for

173

you to win me over, but you didn't have to win me at all Thomas. You won me over with that first smile, and I'll be damned if I leave you now."

Thomas wraps his arms around her, tightly for a moment then slowly loosens his hold, kisses her neck, cheek, and gently, her lips.

"We have to move now." He says. "We have to get to the old barn building. When we do you've got to listen to me. Alright?"

"Okay," she says.

The two sprint off making the journey tree by tree, Thomas leading with Juliandra in tow. He knew the last killer's long range rifle held only six bullets, and so far five have been used. Boon needed his M40 to finish the job, but Thomas's goal is to get there first and stop him. It takes several minutes to reach River Steet, and before emerging from the tree line Thomas slows the pace and tells Juliandra to stay behind the barn while he checks for Boon's whereabouts from a nearby silo. After a few minutes, he begins to think Boon may have beaten them there and could already be inside loading his second rifle. That is until a small reflection of light queues him to look toward a hay building across the road where he catches a glimpse of movement through a window. Thomas immediately turns toward Juliandra to gesture for her to stay put, but when he makes eye contact she starts to run in his direction.

"Stay there!" He yells. "Stop! Go back!"

She makes it almost halfway when suddenly a loud crack fills the air. It was the last bullet from Boon's rifle, and Thomas watches in disbelief as her body spins before falling to the ground. His voice is next to echo out, like a second shot, as he sprints to the twisted figure lying in the grass.

"**No!**" He yells. "Juliandra, are you okay? Juliandra?"

"I think so," she says, "my arm, it hurts, but I think I'm okay."

Thomas exhales in relief, leans forward and kisses her on the forehead. "I love you Juliandra, with all my heart."

Juliandra grabs his shirt and cries out when he begins to stand, but for the first time Thomas pushes her away.

"I love you! I love you, Thomas."

Slowly his head turns in Boon's direction.

"That's six Boon! This is it! You'll never hurt Juliandra or anyone else ever again! You hear me Boon?"

Pieces of grass and particles of dirt fly up creating a temporary trail as Thomas starts running towards the hay building at top speed, maneuvering left and right in a zig zag pattern. Every step seemed to take an eternity and the next wouldn't come fast enough. Each breath was never ending and the air moved around his face as if it was flowing water. He could see Boon walking out, almost in slow motion, reaching for his pistol, and could hear distant sounds of sirens becoming louder and louder as he made his way forward. Thomas accepted his fate. He'd be shot no matter what, but help was on the way, and if Boon could be distracted long enough, Juliandra would live. The crack of a bullet firing rings out, dominating the landscape. Thomas freezes, staring at Boon with surprise, as his body gradually collapses.

There he was lying on the ground motionless. Boon was dead; shot between the eyes with a single bullet. Thomas stood, looking in disbelief.

"What the hell?" He utters.

His body had gone backwards and landed face up, sparking Thomas to turn around, but no one was there. He looks toward the police making their way to him and then again at the barn to see Juliandra walking out holding Boon's second rifle.

"Juliandra?" He says.

She drops the rifle, covers her face and starts to cry.

"I did it." She says. "I finally saved you."

Thomas walks over and embraces her.

"What? What do you mean, **you** finally saved **me**?

"I love you Thomas, I love you." She says while wiping tears from below her eyes. "Thomas, you died. I watched you die. Ten times before today!"

"What? You watched **me** die ten times? That's impossible; I was trying to save you."

"I know. I know what you went through. I know you suffered through my death again and again, and you did everything you could. You did Thomas, you did save me. You sacrificed your life to save mine, right here in front of me. That man shot you with his gun, and you held that gun to yourself, for me. You held it till the police got to you."

"What? That's impossible."

"It's true. The police arrived and you were clutching the gun on your knees. Boon ran off and they chased after him while I held you. You died in my arms, Thomas. I watched your life slip away and when it did, I felt the world stop. Everything was frozen, including us, and then I blacked out. People at the hospital said I was gone until the ambulance crew revived me. I was in the hospital with my mom and Brighten then fell asleep, and when I woke up, I was back home with you as if nothing happened. You jumped out of bed and rushed into the living room just like before. And you ran out of the house just like before. I went to find you just like I did before, and I watched you die right here Thomas, just as before. I didn't understand it. I didn't know what was going on or what to do until one of those mornings I ran into the living and begged you not to go. I knew you'd think I was crazy, but I told you anyway that you were going to die if you left. You kept insisting that you had to leave, to save me. I made you listen. After I explained what was happening, you couldn't believe it. You told me all about what you'd done and needed to do. Then **we** came up with a new idea Thomas. You and I came up with a way to save both of us."

"We did? I don't remember any of this."

"How could you? Each morning is a new start and everything resets and plays out all over. I had to explain everything each morning until our final plan."

"What plan?"

"You made me memorize where the second rifle was in that barn. You insisted I not tell you anything the next morning, and that I let you die as many times as it took. You died ten times Thomas before I was able to shoot that man before he killed you. Ten times!"

Juliandra drops to her knees covering her eyes once again. Thomas kneels down, pulls her close and kisses her repeatedly.

"I love you," he says, "and I believe you, every word. Thank you for saving me."

"You saved me too Thomas, and I will never forget that. You gave your life for me."

As they hold each other an ambulance stops a few feet away and two EMTs rush over.

"Anyone injured here?" One asks.

"Yes," Thomas says, "My wife is. Her left arm."

The second EMT kneels beside Juliandra. "Ma'am, can I take a look at your arm?"

"Of course," she says. "I'm okay, I think I'm okay."

"You're gonna be fine ma'am, but I need to move you into the ambulance so we can clean this up and get some bandages on it before taking you to the hospital. Are you able to stand?"

"She doesn't need to stand," Thomas says, "I'll carry her."

Thomas picks her up and follows the man to the ambulance. Once she's inside he looks at her with a smirk.

"You know I win, right?"

"You win what?" she replies.

"Well, I'm pretty sure I saved you in nine tries, and it took you, umm... What, eleven to save me?"

"Boy! I know you didn't go there! Just for that you're going over to my mom's house while I do her hair! "

Thomas laughs as he climbs in and takes a seat across from her. "Is Brighten gonna be there you think?"

"I don't know, maybe. Why?"

"I think we have some things to talk about."

"Oh?"

"Yeah, I think we're gonna be okay, him and I."

THE END